A THIMBLEFUL OF MURDER

OF

MURDER

A Quilters Club Mystery

Mildred Potter Lissauer, Godey Quilt, 1933-1934.
102 x 91 3/4 inches.
Kentucky Museum, Western Kentucky University.

A THIMBLEFUL OF MURDER

A Quilters Club Mystery

Book 14

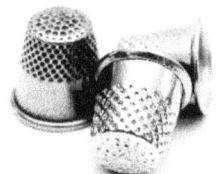

Marjory Sorrell Rockwell

ABSOLUTELY AMAZING eBOOKS

ABSOLUTELY AMAZING eBOOKS

For information contact:
Publisher@AbsolutelyAmazingEbooks.com

ISBN-13: 978-1949504217 (Absolutely Amazing Ebooks)
ISBN-10: 1949504212

"Surely you know what a kiss is?" she asked, aghast.

"I shall know when you give it to me," he replied stiffly, and not to hurt his feeling she gave him a thimble.

- *Peter Pan*, J.M. Barrie

Quilters Club Mysteries

By Marjory Sorrell Rockwell

A Christmas Quit (Prequel)

The Quilters Club Quartet

The Quilters Club Trio

The Underhanded Stitch

The Patchwork Puzzler

Coming Unraveled

Hemmed In

Sewed Up Tight

All Tangled Up

Needled

Stitch In Time

Cross Stitch

Fat Quarters

Stitch in the Ditch

Quilt Block

**Available from
AbsolutelyAmazingEbooks.com**

A THIMBLEFUL OF MURDER

A Quilters Club Mystery

TABLE OF CONTENTS

PART I

Chapter One
The Explosion

Chapter Two
Night Vision

Chapter Three
A Quartet of Jessica Fletchers

Chapter Four
Welcome to the Mansion

Chapter Five
The Quilt in the Back of the Closet

Chapter Six
The Dead Man

PART I

"Would you like an adventure now," he said casually to John, "or would you like to have your tea first?"
                                        - *Peter Pan,* J.M. Barrie

Chapter One

The Explosion

Maddy Madison was thinking that Modigliani or Klee might have made great quilt designers – that is, if they'd worked with fabric instead of paint. These fanciful observations were running through her mind as she examined the patchwork quilts hanging in the new exhibit at the Hoople Quilting Heritage Museum.

That was just before the bomb went off.

The windows in the front of the museum were blown in. Quilts fell off the wall. Brass light fixtures swayed. The building shook like it was experiencing an epileptic seizure. The sound hurt the eardrums.

Actually, it wasn't a bomb – it was a meth lab that blew up.

The lab was located in the house directly across the street. The entire front of that building looked like a fire-blackened cavern. Meth labs are known to be highly flammable, often accidentally blowing up or catching fire.

N-methamphetamine is an addictive stimulant drug that often comes as a white, bitter-tasting powder or a pill. Crystal meth looks like glass fragments or bluish-white rocks. Meth's chemistry is similar to that of amphetamines. Some people like to use the illegal substance as a recreational drug. It's not good for you.

A Thimbleful of Murder

The prevalence of meth labs in the United States is alarming. According to the DEA's National Clandestine Laboratory Register, the state of Indiana tops the list with a reported 1,797 meth labs. How they were able to count these hidden criminal enterprises was a mystery to Maddy.

The apartment belonged to Justin Ford Harribald, a retired history teacher. Fortunately for Mr. Harribald, he had been shopping for groceries when the explosion occurred. Police Chief Jim Purdue picked him up at the Food Lion. The 75-year-old man immediately confessed to operating a meth lab, saying he got the idea from a popular TV show called *Breaking Bad*. It told about a high school teacher who got into the business of "cooking" meth to supplement his income.

Turns out, Justin Harribald had been Maddy's history teacher back in the day.

Bad enough that a respected old educator had turned to the drug trade, but while sifting through the wreckage of Justin Harribald's apartment the firemen discovered a charred body.

~ ~ ~

Maddy's son Freddie was the first responder. As Fire Chief of Caruthers Corners, he'd been on duty that night. Like his men, he kept a schedule of 24 hours on, followed by 48 hours off. A common routine for firefighters, but it played heck with sleep patterns. He could use a dose of melatonin.

Freddie was youngest of her three grown children. Bill was the oldest; Tilly the middle child. In some ways Freddie was Maddy's favorite, her "baby," even though he was now 34. Young for a chief, but his badly scarred face attested to plenty of firefighting experience, gained during his tenure with Atlanta Fire and Rescue.

The fire at the scene of the explosion was minimal. But the front wall had been blown out and that blackened lump he found in the kitchen was a burnt body. The dead man was so badly consumed by the flames you'd think it was a case of spontaneous combustion.

Freddie detected a strong ammonia smell. Like Windex. It made him wrinkle his nose.

Careful to keep his men out of the ruined apartment, he waited for the police to show up. He looked down at the body. Yes, this was definitely a crime scene.

Chapter Two

Night Vision

Maddy's grandson N'yen was pleased with the news that Pluto might be upgraded to planet status again. That earlier diminution had been a blunder by Neil deGrasse Tyson in his opinion – although the astrophysicist remained one of his role models.

Discovered in 1930, Pluto is a thousand times too faint to be seen with the naked eye. It's difficult enough to spot with a telescope, but the boy sat there in one of the gables atop Hoople Mansion, gazing through his 114mm Celestron AstroMaster telescope in the direction he thought Pluto might be.

From the night sky in Indiana you can see seven planets – Mercury, Venus, Mars, Jupiter, Saturn, Uranus, and Neptune. Mercury and Neptune were kinda difficult to see, but the others had good visibility tonight.

There was Mars, a red dot near the Moon. At 35.8 million miles, Mars was the closest it's been to the Earth since 2003.

Astronomy is one of the oldest of the natural sciences. Earlier civilizations such as the Babylonians, Greeks, Egyptians, Chinese, even the Mayans, spent time observing the sky.

From up here at the highest point in the town, 13-year-old N'yen Madison had a bird's eye view of the streets below, a grid defined by pinpoints of lighted homes. It was a beautiful sight, like a reflection of stars in the nighttime sky.

He was planning to check out Asteroid 29 Amphitrite and Asteroid 9 Metis, both visible with a small telescope – but his attention was diverted by a flash down below in the town.

N'yen swung his telescope around and focused on the source of the burst of light. At first he thought it had come from the Hoople Quilting Heritage Museum. The building was brightly lit. His Grammy was at an exhibit there tonight.

But when he spotted the smoke roiling past the street lights, he realized the explosion had come from across the street from the museum. It looked like one of those two-story houses that had been subdivided into apartments.

What was going on down there?

He heard a siren and saw a firetruck pull up in front of the house. Was his Uncle Freddie working tonight? he wondered. Then he saw two police cruisers – his Uncle Jim and one of the deputies. People were starting to pour out of the quilting museum, curiosity seekers ignoring the possibility of another explosion.

Was it a gas main? A terrorist attack? A ruptured pressure cooker?

He searched the surrounding street with his telescope's 20mm eyepiece to see if any cars or runners were leaving the scene, but nothing stood out.

Then he caught a movement, a red car speeding along Second Street, away from the explosion. Was it someone escaping danger? Or fleeing the scene of a crime?

N'yen would have to ask his Grammy what was going on when he saw her at breakfast. The hour was too late for anything to make the morning paper. Too soon to be on the Internet. He closed the window in the gable and padded down the stairs to go to bed.

~ ~ ~

Police Chief Jim Purdue called in a favor from his counterpart in nearby Burpyville, borrowing a forensic crime scene tech – what on television is called a CSI. With its population exceeding 80,000, Burpyville was a city with a greater law enforcement capability than a small middle-of-nowhere town like Caruthers Corners.

About 60% of all US police departments consist of less than 10 full-time officers. Caruthers Corners had even fewer than that.

Burpyville, on the other hand, was big enough for its police department to have specialized departments. In addition to foot patrols and traffic units there was an Investigation Division made up of a Crimes Against People unit, Crimes Against Property unit, Juvenile unit, and Narcotics/Vice unit, plus a well-trained SWAT team and specialized K-9 group. Close to 30 policemen and -women in all.

The Investigation Division was supported by Forensic Services, a section responsible for locating, collecting, preserving, and analyzing physical evidence at crime scenes. This group consisted of a supervisor and two technicians.

Burpyville Police Chief Frank Crenshaw sent his best guy, a ten-year-veteran named Herman Vox. The tech arrived on the scene within two hours of the explosion, not bad timing given the distance between Burpyville and Caruthers Corners. And it wasn't even midnight yet.

Vox was a small guy, maybe 5'2" in his plastic crime scene booties. His Kleenguard A60 Bloodborne Pathogen & Chemical Splash Protection coverall with hoodie made him look like an alien straight from Mars. He wore thick bifocals that caused his eyes to bulge like a bug's. In addition to a Keiser University degree in Criminal Justice, he was a graduate of Homeland Security's Advanced Forensic Techniques In Crime Scene Investigations II (AFTCSI-II) training course. That and plenty on-the-job experience. People said he was good at his work, not fazed by dead bodies or blood or brain tissue splattered on a wall.

This one was what cops called a "crispy critter." Not polite, but very descriptive.

"Anybody been inside?" Vox asked Chief Purdue.

"Just me and the fire chief. I watched where I stepped. When I came across a body, I backed out and called you guys."

"And the fire chief?"

"He knows what he's doing."

"Okay, maybe it's not too badly contaminated." You could tell the little man was fussy about his crime scenes.

"I need to send the Fire Chief back in to determine the cause of the explosion."

"Okay, but he'll need to suit up. I've got another pair of coveralls in the trunk of my car."

"Sure. He's right here."

The forensic tech turn to face a man who looked like Freddy Krueger on a bad day.

"Holy cow. Did you forget to exit a burning building?"

"That about sums it up," said Freddie Madison, his scarred face breaking into a ghoulish grin. Maddy's youngest son was a decorated fireman, appointed as the town's Fire Chief when old Pete Watson retired. With his disfigured countenance, he didn't need to rent a costume at Halloween, he often joked to his friends. He had more or less learned to live with it.

"Okay, suit up and follow me. Try to step where I do."

"Got it."

"This looks like the explosion of a meth lab," Vox said.

"How can you tell?"

"The smell."

~ ~ ~

Three hours later, Vox gave his verbal report.

"Definitely a meth lab explosion. Your fire chief will confirm that. You can smell the ammonia. And we found the remnants of the cooking paraphernalia. Pots, pans, Bunsen burner, a lump of wax, empty ammonia bottles, stuff like that. Explosions are a common phenomenon with these makeshift operations. One little mistake, such as unscrewing the bottle cap too fast, can result in a huge blast. A dangerous profession."

"Guess that body in there testifies to that," said Chief Purdue, taking off his cap to rub his balding dome. "Any idea who it is?"

"Nope. Too burned to be recognizable, no ID left after the fire. But you might get a DNA hit. You could try dentals too. Or wait for somebody to file a Missing Person Report."

"The apartment belongs to a retired schoolteacher, name of Justin Ford Harribald," noted Chief Purdue, glancing down at his clipboard. He kept meticulous notes when it came to a homicide investigation – not that the town had that many.

"That body's not Harribald," said Freddie Madison. "I've seen him around town. This vic is a much bigger guy."

Herman Vox read off the statistics: "About six-foot-two, over two hundred fifty pounds, hair and eyes indeterminate, good teeth with gold fillings, no rings, an expensive wristwatch, work boots based on what was left of them. A wealthy farmer, I'd say. Sound like anybody you know?"

"We don't even know if this was a local guy or an out-of-towner," sighed Jim Purdue. "Maybe if we can find Harribald, he can tell us who was in his apartment."

Chapter Three

A Quartet of Jessica Fletchers

The Quilters Club met every Tuesday in the sewing room at the museum. Maddy was the de facto leader of the group. There were only four members – five if you counted Maddy's granddaughter Aggie. Or six when Maddy's grandson N'yen was in town, not that he pretended to be interested in quilting.

In addition to making patchwork quilts, the four women sometimes got involved in solving crimes. The *Burpyville Gazette* once described them as "a quartet of Jessica Fletchers" – a reference to the amateur detective played by Angela Lansbury on the *Murder, She Wrote* TV show. However, their cases usually involved antique quilts that had been stolen, stuffed with money, or depicting a clue to a mystery. Not so many murders.

Maddy valued the ya-ya sisterhood that had existed between the four women since high school:

– Lizzie Ridenour was the once-glamorous redhead who managed the Hoople Quilting Heritage Museum. Married to a retired bank president, she was by far the best quiltmaker in the whole town. The record showed she'd won the Watermelon Days competition five years in a row.

– Cookie Bentley was the faded blonde beauty

queen who served as executive director of the Caruthers Corners Historical Society. Back in high school, she had been Mr. Harribald's teacher's pet, an escapade she was still living down. Her husband Ben was a retired farmer, the second largest landholder in the county.

– Bootsie Purdue ran the local no-kill animal shelter. The pudgy brunette with the pixie haircut was wife of Police Chief Jim Purdue. Yes, it irked him when the Quilters Club meddled in police business. But Bootsie kept him wrapped around her little finger. He had a thing for voluptuous women.

As for Maddy, she was married to Beauregard Hollingsworth Madison IV, great-grandson of one of the Town Founders. A prestigious position in local society. Back in 1829, Col. Beauregard Madison, Ferdinand Jinks, and Jacob Caruthers had founded the town when the wagon train they were leading got mired down by a broken axel.

Maddy's husband Beau was a former mayor of Caruthers Corners. Now their son-in-law Mark Tidemore held that post. Mark was a shoo-in to be reelected.

On this Tuesday Maddy pulled her fabrics and threads from the pigeonhole in the sewing room's storage wall where they kept their quilting materials. She was working on an Amish design called Drunkard's Path. The pattern allowed her to practice her quilting curves. Piecing together quilt blocks in a Drunkard's Path design starts with aligning the center of the curves. Since the curve on both pieces exposes the bias of the fabric, it's vulnerable to stretching. The trick is to be gentle while handling the curved pieces. Maddy was known to have a good, steady hand.

As for Lizzie, she was finishing up a La Passacaglia Quilt. With its geometric shapes and intricate cutting, this English Paper Piecing design is one of the most difficult quilts to make. The name comes from an old Italian dance tune. Lizzie (née Bergamachi) traced her ancestors back to Italy. Needless to say, she proceeded with ease.

Cookie was tackling a Disappearing Nine Patch. This is a simple variation on the traditional nine-patch block, combining a nine-patch pattern with layer cake fabrics. Cookie pretty well had the hang of it. All left to do was add the broad border.

Bootsie was struggling with an Amish design known as a Bear's Claw. Fairly simple, but quite a task for her. Some people seem to have two left feet; Bootsie had two left hands when it came to sewing pieced quilts.

Across the worktable, 15-year-old Aggie was making progress on a Celtic Knot. The red-and-black design was simple, using only two fabrics on a white background. Celtic knots reminded her of an intertwining Möbius strip. As she worked on the cross stitching, her dog Tige lay sleeping at her feet. The wire-haired dachshund mix usually joined her for these quilting sessions. Faced with school hours, Aggie got only a third as much time on Tuesdays as did the others; she was always playing catch-up.

N'yen sat in a corner of the room playing an interactive Tower Defense game on his iPad. He was locked in a "death struggle" with his avowed nemesis, a gamer known as Beelzebub666. The Devil, as N'yen called him. Beelzebub666 had turned out to be a local guy named Tommy Truehart. Now working as a police deputy, it was puzzling how Tommy found the time to go online so often. He was a formidable opponent, N'yen had to admit.

As usual, gossip mingled with the day's events while the women stitched. It was as if they had fused *The View*, *Entertainment Tonight*, and the *Six O'clock News* to create a hybrid program called *Chatterboxes*. Aggie tried to keep up with the conversation; N'yen mostly tuned them out.

Topic *du jour* – the meth lab explosion, of course.

"That blast certainly disrupted last night's exhibit," Lizzie complained.

"Yes, the party was going well up 'til that point," replied Cookie. "But that big kaboom reverberated like a 6-point-o on the Richter scale!"

"It certainly shook the building," agreed Bootsie. "I spilled my drink."

"I find it hard to believe Mr. Harribald has been making drugs," said Maddy. "He wasn't even a chemistry professor."

"You don't have to know much chemistry to make meth these days," interjected N'yen, without looking up from his iPad. "There's now a simpler method than cooking it over an open flame. However, this new process -- 'Shake and Bake,' it's called – can explode just as easily as the old way."

"How do you know so much about making illegal drugs?" asked his grandmother, glancing worriedly in his direction.

"I read."

"Mr. Know-It-All," Aggie muttered under her breath, but loud enough for him to hear. She and her cousin were at odds this visit. He resented how much time she was spending with her boyfriend instead of him. Despite having a genius level IQ, he still exhibited the emotions of a tween boy.

"Have the police identified the body found in the wreckage?" asked Maddy.

"Not yet," replied Bootsie. As the police chief's wife, she always had the inside track. "The corpse was so badly burned there were no fingerprints left. They're hoping to get a hit on DNA or find dental records that match."

"I hope it's no one we know."

"Don't be silly. We don't know any drug dealers."

"We know Mr. Harribald," Maddy pointed out.

~ ~ ~

"Did the police find that red car?" asked N'yen, not missing a click on his Tower Defense game.

"Red car?"

"Yeah, the one I saw driving away from the explosion last night."

Maddy frowned. "How did you see the explosion? You and Aggie were home watching television."

"Aggie was watching television. Some ol' love story called *Moonrise Kingdom*. About a boy and girl who run off together. I got bored and went up to the gable to look at stars through my telescope."

"But you looked down instead of up?" said Cookie, catching on quick.

"It's almost like looking through my microscope,"

15

he grinned. "People look like amoeba."

"And you saw a red car leaving the scene of the explosion?" pressed Bootsie. This was new evidence that Jim would want to know about.

"Yes. Some kind of Nissan, I think. Hard to tell all those Japanese makes apart. They stamp 'em out with a cookie cutter."

"New or old?" questioned Bootsie, taking notes.

"New, a fancy model."

"You're sure about this?" asked his grandmother.

"I saw what I saw," he replied, continuing his gameplay.

Chapter Four

Welcome to the Mansion

In case you've never been there, Caruthers Corners is a small Indiana town – population 2,812 – located in the northeast corner of the state. The number of residents has gone down quite a bit since that tornado ripped through the town in September. Quite a tragedy. You may have seen the coverage on national news. Aside from the 37 dead, a number of families have moved away to "someplace safer," despite the fact this was the only twister the town has ever experienced in its recorded history.

Nonetheless, Indiana is officially a part of Tornado Alley, that swath of Midwestern states which experience a high number of landspouts, an area stretching from North Texas to Canada.

Forget that Florida ranks Number One among states experiencing tornadoes. Annually it claims 12.2 tornadoes per 10,000 square miles. Indiana is only Number Sixteen – with 6.1 twisters, half as many as the Sunshine State. But people aren't rational about things like that.

The town was beginning to recover from the disaster. The Caruthers Corners Restoration Coalition already had started rebuilding the rows of scenic Victorian homes leveled by the twister. Construction was booming. The economy was starting to bounce back.

~ ~ ~

Since the Madisons' house on Melon Pickers Row had been totally demolished by the 2018 Northeastern Tornado, Maddy and Beau had gone to live with Aunt Hilda in the big stone mansion atop Hoople Hill. They had an entire wing to themselves. Their acceptance of Hilda's hospitality had been influenced by the old lady's announcement that she planned to leave the historic mansion to Maddy. This gave Maddy the opportunity to start enjoying her inheritance in advance.

The place was so big that Maddy's daughter Tilly and her family had been invited to live in another wing. Tilly, her husband Mark, and four children had been made homeless by the twister also. Tilly loved living "in a fairy tale castle." Mark was neutral, since he spent most of his time at the mayor's office in the Town Hall, directing the town's rapid recovery. The three little kids didn't care one way or the other. And Aggie was happy to be near her Grammy and Grampy. All was good.

N'yen had his own suite for visits. Normally, the Asian boy lived in Chicago with his adoptive parents, Bill and Kathy Madison. He was down for a two-week visit with Grammy and Grampy while his parents attended a conference in Colorado. They ran an NGO children's service in the Windy City. Given N'yen's high academic standing, his school had approved the boy's absence. A Sabbatical, they called it.

Aggie thought it sucked that her cousin got a holiday while she still had classes to attend. She and N'yen were both sophomores, being that the 13-year-old boy had skipped two grades in an Advance Placement Program.

Built during the late 1800s by pharmaceutical millionaire Henry Hoople, the three-story stone mansion had served as a summer retreat for his family – wife Henrietta and the world famous Hoople Quadruplets. The 52-room manor contained multiple bedrooms, a formal dining room, well-stocked library, hidden passageways, two elevators, twelve fireplaces, and even a small bowling alley.

The Hoople Quadruplets – Hilda, Howard, Helga, and Helena – had once been as famous as Tom Mix and Rin Tin. Now Hilda was the last of the quadruplets, following the death of Howie – Maddy's biological father.

Maddy liked living in the Hoople Mansion, getting to know her aunt and learn more about her own connection to these quadruplets. Raised as a Taylor, Maddy hadn't known she was adopted until recently.

Discovering her true heritage had turned Maddy's daily existence on its end, revealing that she was the twin sister of Maisie Walters, the woman who ran a local diner called Cozy Café. All her life she'd thought she was an only child.

Hilda Hoople's new factotum, a roly-poly Brit named Marybelle Oliver, ruled this kingdom with the smooth efficiency of a prime minister. Meals were served on time; there was a formal High Tea every afternoon; and the thick wooden front door was locked precisely at 11 o'clock every night. That curfew put some pressure on Aggie's date nights, but she found she could manage if she and Bobby Elwood caught a 7 p.m. showtime at the AMC Multiplex in Burpyville, the nearest movie theater.

~ ~ ~

Bobby Elwood's father had bought him a used Fiat Punto when he turned 16 a few months ago. That meant

A Thimbleful of Murder

Bobby and Aggie weren't tied to double-dating all the time with Prissy Moretz and Teddy DiMacchio. Teddy D recently got himself a hot new car – a loaded, top-of-the-line 2018 Infiniti QX60. He hadn't been seen around town lately. He was probably down in Pitsville visiting Prissy, showing off his new QX60 like a homeboy flashing his bling.

No big deal, Aggie told herself. Bobby's '98 Punto got them to the movies just fine. And it served them well when they wanted some private time. Aggie enjoyed making out with her boyfriend, but she drew the line at hands under clothing or climbing into the backseat. Thankfully, Bobby was (for the most part) a gentleman.

~ ~ ~

N'yen's room was just around the corner from Aggie's in the Mansion. Each of them had a suite consisting of bedroom, private bath, and sitting room. N'yen's space looked more like the laboratory of a mad scientist – filled with computers and telescopes and electronic gizmos. He was particularly proud of his new Zeiss GeminiSEM FE-SEM Electron Microscope. He had discovered the molecular world, becoming fascinated by subatomic particles. The microscope allowed effortless imaging at subnanometer resolution. A $20,000 grant had allowed the boy to purchase a used model.

His intellectual curiosity had switched from the macro (astronomy) to the micro (subatomic structure). He had the makings of a future physicist, his academic advisors said.

"What if atoms are tiny solar systems?" the boy posited to his cousin Aggie.

"What you talkin' 'bout, Willis?" she smart-mouthed him with that catch-phrase from TV's *Different Strokes*.

"Laugh if you like," he brushed her off.

In his astrological studies he'd also come to wonder if our solar system was simply a giant atom. After all, it consisted of a sun in the middle with eight smaller planets orbiting around it ... and the element Oxygen has a nucleus and eight smaller electrons rotating around it in their orbits. One could see a similarity between the two, he insisted.

This was known as the Rutherford-Bohr model, the concept that every atom consists of a nucleus with a certain number of electrons rotating about the nucleus in their orbits like a solar system.

"Our solar system could be similar to Oxygen, while others may be like Chlorine, Iron or Uranium," N'yen postulated. "Perhaps the Universe as seen through telescopes is just the collection of billions of atoms in a larger universe. We could even be atoms in another gigantic living being!"

Aggie wasn't buying it. She was taking Physics 101 this year. "Quantum Mechanics states that electrons, protons, neutrons and the nucleus are probably not tiny spheres, but instead are spread out in the form of a cloud."

"Another theory," he countered, "is that electrons look like tiny strings."

"Fact is, since these particles are too small to be seen in a microscope, what they look like is anybody's guess," retorted Aggie. She didn't like it when he played Mr. High and Mighty.

"True," he admitted.

"I don't like the idea of just being a dot in some giant's butt," said Aggie. "Or a tiny thread on a string."

"More likely you're made up of subatomic strings," he joked. "Maybe that's why your thinking is always tied up in a knot."

That wasn't really true. Agnes Millicent Tidemore had a first-class logical mind – one that helped her solve Quilters Club cases – but lately she had been tied up in knots over her relationship with Bobby Elwood. Was love as complicated as Quantum Mechanics or String Theory?

Chapter Five

The Quilt in the Back of the Closet

On Wednesday morning, Maddy found a strange quilt in the back of a closet in the Madison wing at Hoople Mansion. Making this big stone edifice into their new home had been a challenge. The old house was a repository for a century-and-a-half's detritus. Maddy tried to do a little sorting and tossing each day.

The antique appliqué quilt had been tucked away on a high shelf in the closet of one of the spare bedrooms. The quilt's design was unusual enough to catch her eye, 15 blocks featuring images of stylish women. She'd seen something like this before … but where?

Was this a Godey Quilt?

She had seen pictures of the famous Godey Quilt. Composed of 15 fabric portraits of men and women dressed in fashionable mid-nineteenth century attire, the unique quilt had been created in 1933-1934 by Mildred Potter Lissauer of Louisville, Kentucky. Lissauer's design was not representative of American quilts of that period, a time when standardized patterns and kit quilts were widely available and accepted.

An appliqué is an ornamental needlework in which pieces of fabric are sewn or stuck onto a large piece of fabric to form pictures or patterns.

A Thimbleful of Murder

The Godey Quilt took its name from the appliqués' resemblance to fashion illustrations in the popular 19th-century magazine, *Godey's Lady's Book*. Published from 1830 to 1898, this was the most widely read magazine of the era. Each issue printed advice on home management, rearing children, even poetry. Hand-tinted fashion plates were a popular feature of Louis Godey's publication.

It's true that other pictorial coverlets had preceded the Godey Quilt. Charles Pratt received acclaim for a series of quilts depicting Penn's Treaty (1926). Emma Andres chose 3,630 pieces of silk to make her famous Lady at the Spinning Wheel (1933). And Emma Mae Leonard used eight figural blocks to illustrate a century of women's fashion – 1833 to 1933 – for her entry in the 1933 Century of Progress contest. Yet, Mildred Lissauer's design was unique in that its images were based on newspaper and magazine advertisements, greeting cards, and even playing cards, as the source material.

Martha Potter recorded the start of her daughter's quilt with this straightforward entry in her personal journal:

> *"Mildred started her 'Godey's Ladies.'"*

Thus, the rare quilt's name came into being.

~ ~ ~

The mothball-smelling quilt that Maddy found was also made up of 15 appliquéd blocks, each depicting an attractive lady in her finery. Cookie Ridenour, the historian with an eidetic memory, recognized them as illustrations from *Leslie's Weekly*. At one time it was a competing magazine to *Harper's Weekly* and *Godey's Lady's Book*.

Beginning in 1854 with *Frank Leslie's Ladies' Gazette*

of Fashion, Leslie spun off a publication the following year called *Frank Leslie's Illustrated Newspaper*. Later it morphed into *Leslie's Weekly*, a publication continued by Leslie's widow after his death in 1880. In 1902 it was sold off, remaining in print until 1922.

Lizzie Ridenour was the one who started referring to Maddy's find as the "Frank Leslie Quilt," based on Cookie's identification of the appliqué images. The irony was that "Frank Leslie" was only a made-up name, the penname used by British-born writer and illustrator Henry Carter.

Maddy queried her Aunt Hilda about the provenance of the quilt. "Oh, it's just some old coverlet my mother had. I remember seeing it on a bed in one of the guest rooms when we quadruplets were children. My brother Howie spilled some chocolate on a corner, which is what made my mother put it away. I'd forgotten all about it. If you like it, it's yours."

"We might donate it to the quilting museum," suggested Maddy.

"Oh, the one I funded a couple of years ago? That's a good idea. When you and Aggie look through the house maybe you'll find some other quilts your friend Lizzie would like to have for the museum."

Aggie took this invitation to heart, thinking of it as a Great Treasure Hunt.

~ ~ ~

Enlisting her cousin's assistance, Aggie began the search that very day. School was closed due to a leaky roof. This had been a rainy week. With all the time off, the academic year was likely to be extended way into the summer.

A Thimbleful of Murder

The duo started in the gable of the guest wing and worked their way down, level by level. The mansion's floorplan was laid out as a cross, like the confluence of four townhouses. One wing was occupied by Aunt Hilda and her caregiver. The second was reserved for Grammy and Grampy. Aggie and her three sisters shared the next wing with their Mom and Dad. N'yen had a place in the fourth, the so-called guest wing. Mostly unoccupied, it was easier to start searching there without getting into everybody's personal space.

The old mansion was itself like a museum, filled with assorted clutter and collections. They found cardboard boxes filled with newspaper clippings documenting the public appearances of the Hoople Quadruples (as they were lovingly known). They came upon a closet containing assorted citations and awards. A storage room was crowded with matching clothing – groupings of three dresses and a suit – leftover costumes from their "show biz career," as Aunt Hilda called it.

Additional items they found included a quartet of hobby horses, a scattering of tennis rackets, three magnificent Queen Anne doll houses and a King Arthur castle, dart boards and tea sets, windup trains and building blocks, croquette mallets and wooden balls. Toys galore.

Other rooms were filled with crates of dishes, linens, umbrellas, adult women's clothing, driving gloves and winter mittens, linen tablecloths and knitted doilies, silk bedsheets and goose-down pillows, table lamps and coffee tables, racks of shoes, piles of purses and pocketbooks, and a couple of oil paintings that Aggie suspected might be Old Masters.

All in all, Aggie and N'yen turned up more than two dozen quilts and counterpanes, neatly folded in trunks and smelling of mothballs. Whether any of them might be significant antiques Aggie wasn't qualified to tell. However, none looked anything like the so-called Frank Leslie Quilt.

Tomorrow, she and her cousin would present their finds to the Quilters Club for a more official assessment. Aunt Lizzie knew her quilts. This had been a good day's effort, a perfect rainy day activity, but they were mindful that there remained three more wings to go, not counting the dungeon-like basement.

Chapter Six
The Dead Man

The ID came back on the dead body from the meth lab explosion. The FBI had found no DNA match on CODIS (Combined DNA Index System), but luckily a local dentist – Dr. Randall Orange, DDS – recognized the teeth by the gold filling in a back molar.

"People usually want gold in the front teeth where it shows. Back teeth get porcelain or silver amalgams or composite resins; that's why I remember this one. It belonged to Boyd Aitkens. He said he was rich enough to have gold in *all* his teeth."

"Boyd Aitkens!" exclaimed Police Chief Jim Purdue. "Nobody has reported him missing." Aitkens was the largest landholder in the entire county. He'd bought up parcels for his watermelon farm like there was no bottom to his purse. Aitkens Produce was by far the biggest employer hereabouts, especially if you counted migrant labor.

Boyd Aitkens being dead was bad enough. His body being found in a burned-out meth lab even worse. Was it murder? Or some kind of horrible accident?

And what was a prominent local businessman doing in a drug den in the first place?

"C'mon, Petie. Let's take a ride out to the Aitkens farm and see what's what," said Jim Purdue.

"You got it, Chief," responded Deputy Pete Hitzer, grabbing his cap. The skinny policeman was a stickler for being in uniform. He took his job in law enforcement seriously. "Wanna take my cruiser?"

"Sure," said the Chief. Petie's car was always spic and span. He washed it twice a week. Jim's car usually had a few hamburger wrappers on the passenger seat. Cozy Café next door made great burgers to go. Jim's growing paunch was an uncontested testament to that.

On the way out to the Aitkens farm, Petie asked, "If that dead man is Boyd Aitkens, who will take over his watermelon business? His wife died a few years back. So did his son Charlie."

"Dunno about his will. But his other son – Ralph, I think his name is – has been foreman at the farm for the last ten or fifteen years."

"Yeah, I know Ralph. He's a loudmouth, always bragging how wealthy his old man is. Guess he's gonna become Richie Rich now."

"I expect you're right. Don't know who else Boyd would leave it to."

"Didn't Mayor Tidemore write up Boyd's will?"

"Yeah, I think he did." Mark Tidemore had been a lawyer before becoming the town's mayor. He'd been known as Mark the Shark in the courtroom.

"Be nice to know who benefits, just in case this turns out to be murder."

"*Cui bono* – that's the phrase."

"Chief, you know I don't speak French."

"Hang on a minute." Jim Purdue fished out his iPhone and dialed a number. He asked to speak with the Mayor. Used to the police chief's daily calls, Mark's secretary put him straight through.

"What's up, Jim?" came the familiar voice.

"Y'know that dead body in the meth lab? Looks like it was Boyd Aitkens."

"Jeez, that's terrible." The watermelon farmer was a prominent citizen, even served on the Town Council. "Are you sure about this?"

"Dr. Orange identified the teeth."

"This is really bad news. What was he doing in a meth lab?"

"Dunno. Me and Petie are on the way to Aitkens Produce. Guess we'll talk with Ralph. Maybe he can tell us something. But in the meantime I wondered if you could tell me about Boyd's will. Does Ralph inherit the farm?"

"No, he doesn't. That's going to surprise a few people. Boyd's daughter Suzy gets it all."

"Suzy? I didn't know he had a daughter. I thought his son Ralph was his only heir. The other boy, Charlie, died a few years back."

"Boyd kept it a secret. Suzy's a love child with a woman down in Pitsville."

"No kidding?"

"I suppose there's no harm in letting the secret out now that Boyd's dead. Suzy will be inheriting everything."

"That's going to shock a few folks. Especially Ralph."

"Yes, I expect it will," said the mayor. "But the question remains, what was Boyd doing at a meth lab? Far as I know, Boyd didn't drink, smoke, or do drugs."

"He was a big churchgoer too, a member of St.

Paul's United."

"If he was so danged religious, what was he doing having a baby outta wedlock?" muttered Petie Hitzer. The Chief had his iPhone on Speaker Mode.

"That fling took place after his wife passed away," replied the mayor. "He got one of his office workers pregnant. She moved back to Pitsville, but Boyd stepped up to the plate and supported mother and daughter. Set up a college fund for Suzy. Tried to do right by her. When his son Charlie got killed, he had me change his will. Left everything to the girl."

"Well, I'll be," said Chief Purdue as the cruiser made the turn into the Aitkens farm. Tires splattering the mud puddles. "I didn't see that coming."

~ ~ ~

Ralph Aitkens was shocked to hear that his dad might be dead. "That can't be right. He left town on a business trip," Ralph insisted. "He drove over to Vincennes to meet with the Illiana Watermelon Association. He's on the board of directors."

"You haven't heard from him since he left?" asked Chief Purdue.

"No, but he rarely calls in. Not unless he's got some marching orders for the crews."

"Did he ever mention a man by the name of Justin Harribald?"

Ralph screwed up his face to think. "Not that I recall."

"Ralph, I'm sorry to tell you this, but your dad was killed when a meth lab in Justin Harribald's apartment exploded. He probably died instantly, didn't suffer."

"A meth lab –?"

"Yeah, it seems that Mr. Harribald – a retired high school teacher – was making a little money on the side."

"What did that have to do with my dad?"

"That's what we're trying to find out."

~ ~ ~

Vincennes is located on the lower Wabash River in the southwestern part of Indiana, about halfway between Evansville and Terre Haute. Founded in 1732 by French fur traders, Vincennes is the oldest continually-inhabited European settlement in Indiana and one of the oldest settlements west of the Appalachians. The fort was named after a French explorer and soldier, Francois-Marie Bissot, Sieur de Vincennes.

Funnyman Red Skelton was born in Vincennes. Tourists like to visit the Red Skelton Museum of American Comedy on the campus of Vincennes University. It displays memorabilia from the comedian's longtime radio, TV, and movie career.

Also the town was site of the first Catholic Church in Indiana (1749), home of the first newspaper in Indiana (1804), the first bank in Indiana (1814), first county hospital in Indiana (Good Samaritan Hospital, 1908), and the very first post office.

Less noticeable is the headquarters of the Illiana Watermelon Association, an organization designed to unite melon farmers in Illinois and Indiana. Boyd Aitkens, being the biggest watermelon producer in Caruthers County, held a position on the board.

Chief Jim Purdue's phone call confirmed that Aitkens had not been there this week.

"Boyd's dead, you say?" gasped an association member. "I can't believe it."

"When's the last time you saw him?"

"It's been about two months since last time he came down to visit us. But I spoke with him on the phone a week or so ago."

"About what?"

"He had some suggestions about the annual convention that's coming up in March at the French Lick Springs Hotel Resort. This is its 30th year."

"Suggestions?" Chief Purdue came from the Joe Friday "few words" school of questioning. Friday was the just-the-facts cop on TV's *Dragnet*.

"About the competition to pick the IWA Queen," explained the member.

"You have a queen?"

"Yes indeed. Each year we select a new Queen at our Annual Watermelon Convention from a slate of candidates from across our district. She becomes a Promotional Ambassador for our association for the upcoming year, making appearances at Welcome Centers, county and state fairs, parades, festivals, and schools to promote the watermelon industry."

"What kind of suggestions did Boyd have?"

"He wanted to increase the Wardrobe Allowance. The competition isn't a beauty contest, but we want our Queen to present herself well. That's an important part of representing our association – that she dress well."

So Ralph Aitkens was wrong about his dad going out of town.

Chapter Seven

A Pile of Quilts

"Y ou've certainly turned up some fine old quilts," nodded Lizzie Ridenour as she examined the youngsters' discoveries. "But nothing as unique as that Frank Leslie Quilt your grandmother found. That one still requires some research, but I believe it might have historical significance in the quilting world."

They had met at the quilting museum to examine their finds – an assortment of patchworks that ranged from Amish Wedding Quilts to Crib Quilts to Crazy Quilts – 27 by actual count. Aggie and N'yen had ridden over with their Grammy, the stacks of quilts filling the rear seat of Maddy's new Navigator.

Aggie's dog Tige got to stay home, rather than risk him tracking up the polished wooden floor in the museum gallery. The rain was still coming down, like that "When it rains it pours" motto on a Morton's Salt box. Mudpuddles spotted the ground like pools of spilt chocolate milk.

"Who was Frank Leslie?" asked Aggie. She had never heard of the guy.

"He was actually an illustrator – worked with woodblock engravings mostly – who became a publisher back in the 1800s," explained Cookie, the historian with a super memory for facts.

35

"How does he have anything to do with the quilt Grammy found?" asked N'yen.

"The appliqué images on the quilt are based on pictures from his magazine, *Leslie's Weekly*," said Lizzie. "Your Aunt Cookie recognized them. That's why we tagged it the 'Frank Leslie' quilt."

"But what makes it historically important?"

"Because it predates a famous quilt known as the Godey Quilt," explained his grandmother.

"How do we know that?"

Maddy pointed to a corner of the Frank Leslie Quilt. "Look, it has the year 1925 stitched here. That's likely the date it was made. And we know Mildred Lissauer didn't start working on the Godey Quilt until 1933."

"Was there a Mr. Godey too?" asked Aggie. Her curiosity moving from Frank Leslie to Godey. All these names were new to her. The weekly Quilters Club meetings had taught her a lot about sewing, but not much about the history of quilting. Or magazines.

"Yes, Louis Antoine Godey," confirmed Cookie. "He was a newspaper boy who worked his way up to becoming a wealthy publisher in Philadelphia. *Godey's Lady's Book* was America's first successful women's fashion magazine. Even bigger than *Leslie's Weekly*."

"Really?"

"At one time *Godey's Lady's Book* was the most widely circulated magazine in America, reaching 150,000 by 1858. People called it 'Queen of the Monthlies,' " confirmed Cookie. Facts tumbling out of her memory banks like confetti.

"Another interesting tidbit," added Lizzie. "Louis

Godey hired a woman named Sarah Josepha Hale to be the editor of *Godey's Lady's Book*. She was famous for writing the poem, 'Mary Had a Little Lamb.' "

"I thought that was an old nursery rhyme," frowned Aggie.

"It was, but based on Hale's poem."

"Here's another fact for you," interjected Cookie. "Mrs. Hale's poem was the first audio recording ever made by Thomas Edison on his newly invented phonograph."

Aggie was impressed; N'yen not so much. "Paul McCartney recorded his own version of 'Mary Had a Little Lamb,'" noted the boy. "It became a Top 20 hit in England."

"How do you know that?" asked Cookie. "You were born 32 years *after* Paul McCartney's 1972 Wings summer tour."

"I listen to music," he said defensively. "I subscribe to Spotify."

~ ~ ~

In May 1934, Mildred Lissauer's mother had suggested she enter the Godey Quilt in some contests. A letter written fourteen months later confirms she did that. "I am glad you brought home the bacon with it," her mother acknowledged its win.

Cookie continued her litany: "We know the Godey Quilt also won an honorable mention at the 1939 National Home Show Quilt and Coverlet Exhibition in Louisville. A local newspaper observed that it had never been exhibited without winning a prize."

"At the time the quilt was valued at $5,000," noted Lizzie. "That's an almost unheard of figure for a quilt back then." She'd obviously been doing some homework to keep up with the blonde historian.

"That's amazing," responded Cookie. "Because Mildred Lissauer didn't do any of the quiltmaking herself. The designs were sketched onto the fabric by her husband and she hired three professional quiltmakers to stitch and stuff the quilt for her."

Aggie looked puzzled. "How can Mrs. Lissauer be famous for a quilt she didn't really make?"

"Andy Warhol didn't personally do his silkscreen paintings," shrugged her cousin. "He just called up his printer and said, 'Let's do a silkscreen of Mao Tse-tung in blue."

"Really?" replied Bootsie. She recognized Warhol as a famous artist, but didn't know much about the Pop Art Movement.

N'yen had more: "And Thomas Kinkade didn't paint those pictures of cozy little cottages in the forest all by himself. He merely gave his mass-produced paintings a brushstroke or two so he could claim them as his own – and then signrd his name at the bottom."

"That's shocking," exclaimed Maddy. She was a traditionalist at heart.

"One in every twenty American homes owns a copy of one of Thomas Kinkade's paintings," the boy added.

"Hey, I own a Thomas Kinkade," exclaimed Lizzie. "Are you telling me it's not real?"

"The signature is," grinned N'yen.

"Can we get back to the quilts?" said Cookie. As a historian she had little interest in any paintings that followed the 1913 Armory Show. Known as the International Exhibition of Modern Art, it was the first large exhibition of modern art in America. She preferred the old stuff – painters like Michelangelo, da Vinci, Rembrandt, Watteau, even Thomas Cole and John Singleton Copley.

"Sorry," said Aggie. "I'm still trying to figure out how Mildred Lissauer got famous for a quilt she didn't make."

"Because she *conceived* of it," replied Lizzie. But it didn't sound like a very convincing argument. Maybe she was trying to justify the authenticity of her Kinkade painting.

"Mildred Lissauer came up with a pictorial appliqué quilt based on magazine illustrations at a time when that wasn't the prevailing style," explained Cookie. "It was a first – until we found a similar quilt dated eight years earlier."

"The Frank Leslie Quilt?"

"Right," confirmed the redhead. "It's a really big deal."

"We know a lot about the Godey Quilt," said Bootsie. "But what do we know about our Frank Leslie Quilt?"

"Not much yet," admitted Maddy. "We don't even know who to credit for making it."

Chapter Eight

Suzy Q

Susan Quinlan Aitkens – Boyd's name appeared on her birth certificate, so she officially took his surname – drove up to Caruthers Corners to meet with the estate attorney. When Mark Tidemore became mayor, he'd turned his practice over to Harlan Elkins Dingley – a young lawyer fresh out of the Yale Law School. Mark had worked with Harlan's grandfather, the late Bartholomew Dingley, Esq.

Because Mark had drawn up the original will, he agreed to meet with Harlan Dingley and Boyd's daughter. A matter of courtesy, clarifying any questions that might come up. Ralph would be there too. So he knew it could get contentious.

As it turned out, Ralph Aitkens brought along his own lawyer, a shyster named J. Harold Wentworth. Wentworth's license to practice law was in the process of being revoked by the Indiana State Bar Association. The ambulance chaser had been convicted of illegally dipping into his escrow accounts. Fourteen counts of embezzlement in total. But that malfeasance wasn't an issue with Ralph. He subscribed to the "It Takes a Crook ..." theory of lawyering.

Harlan Dingley was pretty wet behind the ears. He looked about 17 years old, a slender young man with a baby face and curly brown hair. But the Yale degree attested to his qualifications.

Suzy Aitkens was a "cutie," as Harlan would later describe her to his friends – emerald-green eyes and tousled black hair, as attractive as a girl you might see on a John Deere calendar. She seemed confused by this meeting, having no idea that she'd been named in her late father's will.

As for Wentworth, he was a handsome enough fellow but starting to look a bit seedy, his suit slightly wrinkled and the hint of a paunch showing beneath his starched white shirt. He didn't impress you as a guy you'd let hold your watch.

On the other hand, Ralph Aitkens was a hulking hayseed of a guy, looking the part of a farmer in his faded overalls and plaid flannel shirt. A sycophantic son who'd spent his life trying to please daddy, he looked as if he'd finally realized his failure to do so.

Mark the Shark was in his element. A Harvard grad, he'd played in the Big Leagues for a high-powered Los Angeles law firm before returning home and morphing into a successful political career. He'd won the mayor's post by a landslide. Reelection was predicted to be a snap due to his immense popularity. His leadership following the recent tornado disaster had won him many accolades.

"Harlan, how are you?" the mayor greeted Harlan Dingley. He considered the young lawyer to be his protégé ... just as he'd been Bartholomew Dingley's protégé back in the day. The old man had helped him get into Harvard Law School. He was glad to see Harlan following in his grandfather's footstep, even if he'd picked Yale over Harvard. The boy had the making of a good attorney. The town needed one.

Johnny Wentworth lived in Burpyville, but he'd grown up in Caruthers Corners. Mark Tidemore remembered him as being a bully and cheat in high school. He'd got his law degree from Thomas M. Cooley Law School, an institution ranked as the "worst law school in the country."

"Just fine, Mark. I sure appreciate your sitting in on this reading of the will."

"Least I could do, since I wrote it. Boyd was pretty clear to me about his wishes."

"If he cut me out, there'll be hell to pay," growled Ralph. He was in a foul mood, even before the will was read. Mark didn't expect his mood would get any better once he heard its provisions.

"Don't worry," sneered J. Harold Wentworth. "We'll break this cockamamie will if we have to."

"The document reflects Boyd Aitkens' last wishes," replied Mark. A statement of fact. As for Wentworth's aspersions about the will, that was just bluster to impress his client.

"Last wishes – that doesn't matter. Boyd Aitkens hasn't been in his right mind for years. Ralph here actually ran the family enterprise. His old man was just a figurehead."

Mark didn't bother to respond. He knew a *non compos mentis* charge wouldn't stick. Everybody in town could testify to Boyd's soundness of mind. Just last week the watermelon farmer gave a talk at the Rotary Club that drew high praise. There was no indication of diminished capacity.

"Why don't we get down to business before you start making threats," Harlan Dingley suggested in a calm voice. He looked amused by his opponent's theatrics. This was a simple disbursement of assets to a beneficiary. Mark Tidemore had been named as executor. This will would be difficult to contest.

"Okay, let's get to it," said Ralph. "But first, who the heck is this woman? What's she doing here?"

"This is Suzy Aitkens," Harlan introduced the twentysomething woman. "She's your sister."

"What? I don't have no sister. There was just me and my brother Charlie – and he's dead."

Mark spoke up. "I hate to be the one to tell you, Ralph, but your father had a few secrets. Suzy here is the love child between Boyd Aitkens and Marlene Jurgens. This affair took place several years after your mother passed away. Suzy is their progeny."

"I remember Marlene Jurgens," snorted Ralph. "She used to work in the front office for Aitkens Produce. Don't tell me my dad banged her?"

"Hey –!" said Suzy. Clearly she was not going to allow him to disparage her mom.

"Everybody calm down," advised Harlan Dingley. "Let's try to conduct ourselves with some civility."

"This girl is illegitimate," charged Wentworth. "She has no claim on the Aitkens estate.

"To the contrary," responded Mark Tidemore, "Boyd Aitkens acknowledged Suzy as his daughter, supported her, put her through college, and named her in his will as sole heir."

"He didn't put *me* through college," bemoaned Ralph. "I went to work on the farm straight outta high school."

"Boyd told me you didn't have the grades to get into college. That you even got rejected by Burpyville Community." Everybody knew BCC was the easiest school in the state for a student with poor grades to get accepted.

"That don't matter. I'm the first born," boasted Ralph Aitkens. "That gives me the birthright."

Mark ducked his gaze with obvious discomfort. "I'm sorry to break it to you this way, Ralph, but Boyd told me he was not your actual father. That you were the product of an affair between your mother and a local schoolteacher named Justin Ford Harribald."

"Say, isn't that the guy your police chief arrested for having a meth lab," interjected Wentworth.

"That's right. The lab was in Harribald's home. That's where Boyd Aitkens died in an explosion."

"You're saying my dad wasn't my dad?" Ralph's voice broke. Tears swelled in his eyes. He was either distraught or a very good actor.

Mark shrugged. "That's what he told me. I believed him. But you might want to consider a DNA test to clear up any doubt. Like I said, I'm sorry you had to find out this way. I'd hoped Boyd would have shared this information with you."

"You sure about this?" wailed Ralph, sounding like a wounded bull facing off against a matador. "He never told me a word. He was always a little distant, but I just thought it was because Charlie was his favorite."

"A-are you saying Ralph and I aren't blood relatives?" sputtered Suzy. Looking confused by the onslaught of new information. Apparently her father hadn't told her much either.

"Technically, no. Boyd was your father, but not Ralph's."

"Now see here –!" J. Harold Wentworth shouted. But he wasn't quite sure where to go from there. He hadn't foreseen this turn of events.

"Hold on, everybody," insisted Harlan Dingley. "You came here for a reading of the will. Let's get that over with before getting into a shouting match."

There was some grumbling, but the attendees settled into the vinyl chairs that circled Dingley's desk.

"I'm going to read it to you word for word," said the young lawyer, "but the bottom line is that Susan Quinlan Aitkens gets everything."

"And I get bupkus?" cried Ralph Aitkens. "That's not fair. I helped build that farm into the largest in the county."

"Don't worry," scowled Wentworth. "Like I told you, we'll break this stupid will."

"I doubt that," commented Mark the Shark. He knew how to write ironclad agreements and unbreakable last will and testaments. Boyd's last wishes were unassailable.

"We'll see you in court!" threatened Johnny Wentworth. More of a bully than barrister.

"Wait a minute," Suzy halted them with a raised hand. "Stop shouting. I'm willing to share the estate with Ralph. I don't know anything about watermelons. I need him to run the farm. And he needs me to protect his interests. Our dad could be a hard, unforgiving man. But Ralph is no more responsible for his parentage than I am for mine."

And thus a détente was reached.

Chapter Nine

The Suspect With a Red Car

Chief Purdue assigned Myrtle Doppler, the police dispatcher, to contact Citizens Telephone about any calls to or from Boyd Aitkens the night he died. That was the carrier for his land lines. He used AT&T for his iPhone. She'd tackle them next.

Results were that nothing of consequence turned up with either carrier. The afternoon of his death he'd called a fertilizer supplier in Indianapolis. His son Ralph had called him. And there had been a robo call from a political candidate for State Senate. The November election was coming up in a few days.

~ ~ ~

Acting on N'yen Madison's tip, the Chief had one of his deputies check on any red cars associated with Aitkens or his acquaintances. Tommy Truehart was a computer whiz, so he easily accessed the records of the Bureau of Motor Vehicles (BMV) and then checked all security cameras in the area of the meth lab explosion. Taking a cue from big cities like London, most of the security cameras in town were hooked up to an online network, accessible if you had the proper password. The police department did, but Tommy could have hacked it if need be. Beelzebub666 was quite proficient in his computer skills.

Unfortunately, there were way too many red cars registered in Caruthers Corners for the search to be useful. All the Aitkens Produce vehicles happened to be red, kind of a brand identity – Watermelon Red, the shade was called. His son drove a company car, a Chevy. His daughter owned a red car, a Mustang. Even the lawyer representing Ralph had a red car, an older-model Buick. Unfortunately, the Asian boy hadn't been able to positively identify the make, only catching sight of the fleeing vehicle for a second or two. But he'd thought it might be a Nissan, a high-end model like an Infiniti.

The security cameras were more helpful. Deputy Truehart checked all the businesses along Second Street, where the Madison boy had spotted the car. He trusted N'yen's observational skills. Having played online games with him for the past year, he had great respect for the kid's intellect and acuity. N'yen's latest online avatar was called Hawkeye748.

The camera covering the US Post Office's parking lot caught a fuzzy image of a Nissan Infiniti, date stamped 21:47. The explosion took place precisely at 9:43 p.m., according to the witnesses at the quilting exhibit across the street. And four minutes was about the right amount of time to get from there to where Second Street crossed Fourth Avenue at the Post Office.

Although a block away, caught in the background of a parking lot panorama, Tommy Truehart could make out a 2018 Nissan Infiniti despite the grainy black-and-white image. The shade of gray looked about right to be red. He couldn't make out the driver. Moving fairly fast, the car's details were a little blurred.

Now, having determined the make and model, the deputy crosschecked that with his vehicle registration list. There it was, only one red 2018 Nissan Infiniti in Caruthers County. The registration was in the name of Theodore Arturo DiMacchio, age 17.

Tommy Truehart knew Teddy D. He'd heard the boy had recently dropped out of school. His father's business had been wiped out by the tornado, which begged the question as to where Teddy D got the money for a fancy ride like this. A 2018 Infiniti QX60 commanded a sticker price of $43,300 without any frills or add-ons. That was more than Tommy Truehart made in a year as a deputy! And certainly more than a high school drop-out could pull down, what with Pizza Hut and Dollar General paying only $8 an hour.

~ ~ ~

Chief Purdue was pleased with Deputy Truehart's progress. "Let's pull Teddy D in for questioning. Probably the scuzzball was simply joyriding in the wrong neighborhood, but we need to check it out."

"You got it, Chief."

"Anything else?"

"Not yet. I helped Myrtle check the Aitkens phone records. Nothing there, far as I could see," said the deputy. "But I haven't looked at his email yet."

"Forget it," said the police chief. "A waste of time. Boyd's death is going to go down as a tragic accident. All we gotta do is figure out what he was doing in a meth lab. And I expect we'll get the answer to that when Justin Harribald starts talking."

"He's not saying anything?"

"No, but he will. When I threaten to drop a manslaughter charge on him, he'll sing like a crow."

"Uh, crows don't sing."

"Crow, canary – you know what I mean."

Chapter Ten

Four Birth Certificates

Aunt Hilda Hoople was getting a little dotty – probably an offshoot of her advancing Parkinson's Disease. In addition to the telltale palsy, one symptom of Parkinson's can be hallucinations and confusion.

Today, she disappeared.

That wasn't remarkable in a 52-room mansion. Lots of places to wander off, out of sight. The video system at the front door showed she hadn't left the building.

Aggie thought this could be more of a challenge than looking for stored-away quilts. It had taken her and N'yen a full day to search the guest wing. They hadn't even got to the other three sections of the big house yet. Now they had to find Aunt Hilda before she fell and hurt herself or panicked at being lost in her own home. Marybelle was calm about the search, but you could tell she was worried by the furrowed brow.

Tilly had to watch the Trio of Trouble (as Aggie called her younger sisters). That left a search party comprised of Maddy, Beau, Aggie, N'yen, and Marybelle. They divided up the house, each getting a wing. Marybelle took Aunt Hilda's annex, Beau took the Madison side, Maddy took her daughter's section, and N'yen took the guest extension where his rooms were located. Aggie took the basement.

Her mom might think of the mansion as a fairy tale castle, Aggie viewed the basement as a dungeon. Years ago she's been in one sector of the basement, when she and her cousin slid down the old coal chute and got trapped down there. The lower level of the mansion was like a Minotaur's labyrinth, a confusing collection of meandering hallways and closed-off rooms. It would be very easy for someone – Aunt Hilda, for instance – to get disoriented down there.

Despite the basement's spooky atmosphere, Aggie bravely probed the shadows with her flashlight. Apparently a fuse had blown since she was last down here, leaving this underworld in total darkness. She had to admit, she was a little bit scared even with Tige at her heels.

Aggie was methodical about her search, not wanting to miss Aunt Hilda if she'd wandered down here. Room on the left, clear. Room on the right, clear. Next room on the left, clear. And so on.

By accident she stumbled onto the fuse box in a far corner of a utility room. It was well-labeled, one switch identified as BASEMENT. "Let there be lights," she shouted as if offering a mystical incantation. She flipped the switch and a number of basement lightbulbs glowed like a newly created constellation.

"That's better," she said aloud. Her voice affording her some small sense of comfort.

She continued her search with the benefit of overhead lighting. The old furnace room was foreboding. The mini-bowling alley looked forlorn. A ping-pong room with a sagging table seemed forever abandoned.

As Aggie entered another section of the basement, something caught her eye in a room with an open door. A big boxy object. A refrigerator? No, it was a safe. A big double-door steel safe like you'd see in a bank in a cowboy movie. Across its front the painted words proclaimed HERRING-HALL-MARVIN SAFE CO. This 2-ton lockbox stood about 70-inches tall. It certainly looked impregnable.

Fascinated by the discovery, she walked over to examine the safe's circular combination lock. To her surprise, one of the thick doors was open a crack. What was the point of having a safe if you didn't lock it, she told herself.

Swinging the heavy doors open, she encountered shelves stacked with a hodgepodge of papers and ledgers. Curious, she thumbed through them. Deeds, bank statements, invoices stamped PAID. But no stock certificates, no stacks of hundred-dollar bills, no jewelry. Oh well.

She started to shut the thick steel doors when she noticed a square rosewood box labeled BIRTH CERTIFICATES. That caught her attention. Lifting the wooden lid, she peeked inside. But rather than being birth certificates for the Hoople Quadruplets, the documents merely referred to Girl 1, Girl 2, Girl 3, and Boy 1. Each bore a red-ink stamp that said REV. DAVID DIMPLEDORF'S CARING HOME FOR UNWED MOTHERS.

Odd.

~ ~ ~

Aunt Hilda turned up in the pantry on the first floor. "I was looking for some tea biscuits," she explained innocently. "I wanted something to nibble on when I had my Chamomile at bedtime."

Never mind that bedtime was eight hours away.

Marybelle took the hint and prepared a pot of tea for the whole family. High Tea came early today. She produced a package of McVitie's Simply Classic Rich Tea Biscuits to go with the cuppa. Specially stocked for Aunt Hilda by Food Lion, McVitie's was the old woman's favorite cookies.

Aggie was all fidgety as she sipped her tea. "What's with you?" her mother asked. "You act like you have ants in your pants."

"I don't think that's very likely, unless she sat on an anthill," said N'yen. He'd never heard the expression before, so he took it literally.

"Sorry," said Aggie. "I'm simply perplexed over something I found in the basement."

"Well, it certainly wasn't me," declared Aunt Hilda. "I was in the pantry looking for these tea biscuits." She held one up as Exhibit A. "Very tasty – they're imported from England, I'm told."

"No, I found a big old safe."

"Oh that," chuckled Aunt Hilda. "I keep important papers in it."

"It was unlocked."

Aunt Hilda waved the comment away. "I keep it unlocked because I forgot the combination years ago."

"Then what's the value of having a safe?" asked N'yen. The incongruity baffled him.

"That old safe belonged to my parents. It's merely a good place to store stuff. There are plenty of shelves inside it."

"It was certainly filled with papers," agreed Aggie. "But I found a box that puzzled me. It held birth certificates with no names on them."

"My goodness. You shouldn't be looking at them. Those birth certificates are the Family Secret."

"Family secret?" said Maddy. "What family secret?"

Aunt Hilda looked distressed. "Maddy dear, there are things no one should ever know. Just forget I mentioned it."

Maddy turned to her granddaughter. "Aggie, would you and N'yen go down and fetch that box – the one with the old birth certificates?"

"N-no!" protested Aunt Hilda.

"Look now," said Marybelle protectively, "you're upsetting her."

"Aunt Hilda, we should have no family secrets," said Maddy, patting her hand. Trying to soothe her.

The elderly woman stopped moaning and took a deep breathe. "Oh my. I guess the cat's out of the bag. It will be such a disappointment to the world."

"What?" said Tilly. Wondering if she should cover the little children's ears.

"The birth certificates, I should have burned them years ago," declared Aunt Hilda. She sat up a little straighter, like a prisoner bravely facing execution. "But they were my only connection to the truth."

"What truth?" insisted Maddy."

"That we Hoople Quadruplets weren't actually brother and sisters."

Chapter Eleven

A Circus Side Show

Had the old woman completely lost her mind? The idea that the World Famous Hoople Quadruplets weren't related to each other was too weird to be believed. The foursome had been on the front page of every major newspaper, made appearances all over the world, met with kings and queens. They had been – celebrated!

Maddy said, "How could you *not* be brother and sisters? You're quadruplets."

"Alas, it was all a sham," sighed Hilda Hoople. "Just a side show act. Like something P.T. Barnum would have concocted. Human Fiji Mermaids – not real."

"Aunt Hilda, you're letting your imagination run away with you. Take a deep breath and try to calm down."

"I'm calm. And what I say is true."

"There, there," tsk'ed Marybelle Oliver. "Parkinson's will play tricks on your mind, dearie."

"My mind's just fine, thank you very much," the old woman barked. "Why won't any of you believe me?"

Just then Aggie and N'yen came tromping up the basement steps, Tige galloping a few feet behind them. Aggie was carrying a square wooden box in her arms like a high priestess delivering sacraments. An ornate container, its surface was carved with an intricate design of intersecting flower petals.

Aggie carefully sat the box on the dining room table, the reddish rosewood a sharp contrast against the white linen tablecloth. Aunt Hilda stared at it as if confronting a gift from Pandora. N'yen stood next to Aggie like an honor guard. Beau and Tilly sat back, like birds mesmerized by a snake. The little children ran off, playing chase. Tige went barking after them.

Finally Maddy spoke: "This is your box of private papers, the Family Secret you call it. I think it's time to confront it. But I won't open the box if you don't want me to."

"Oh, go ahead. Let the burden of the secret be yours. I've carried it far too long. After I lost Howie and my sisters, the entire weight fell onto my frail shoulders."

Maddy hesitated, then lifted the lid of the box. Just as Aggie had foretold, there were four yellowed birth certificates stamped at top with REV. DAVID DIMPLEDORF'S CARING HOME FOR UNWED MOTHERS. The certificates were made out to Girl 1, Girl 2, Girl 3, and Boy 1 – each endorsed with a different mother's name.

Ohmygod, thought Maddy. Could it be true – that the so-called Hoople Quadruplets *were* adopted?

~ ~ ~

They sorted through the papers carefully. Four birth certificates. And in the bottom of the box, beneath the documents, they found a scrap of paper with the scribbled message: SECRET PAPERS IN VAULT.

"That doesn't make sense," said Aggie. "Aunt Hilda said *these* birth certificates were the Family Secret."

"Is that right, Miss Hoople?" gently prodded Marybelle. "Are those the Family Secret – that you quadruplets weren't brother and sisters?"

"Y-yes," mumbled the old woman. "But seems like there were more papers, I don't remember what."

"She's getting tired," cautioned Marybelle Oliver.

"No matter," said Maddy. "This is a big enough bombshell."

"Maybe this note is just a reminder to keep these papers locked in the safe," Aggie speculated.

"Or maybe there are more papers at the bank," tried N'yen.

"One thing at a time," said Maddy, taking a deep breath. She was finding the world changing around her faster than she could assimilate it. She felt like she might faint. "I need to get my head around this. If the Quadruples aren't really Hooples, who am I?"

Then she felt Beau's hand on her shoulder and the moment of panic passed.

What to do now? She needed to speak to Barnabas Soltairé. As executive director of Hoople Quadruplets Trust Fund, he needed to be informed of this startling revelation.

Chapter Twelve

The Family Fixer

Barnabas Soltairé still maintained a fancy office in Indy. The former Mob lawyer was a high roller with expensive tastes. A few years back, he had quit working for Salvatore Milano to oversee the Hoople Quadruplets Trust Fund. A personal obligation, in that his mother had worked for the Hoople family. And because the Hooples had put him through law school. Nonetheless, he and Sal the Whisperer remained on good terms. The old mobster thought of him as a misguided nephew.

"He'll come back," Sal told his consiglieri. "The money's too good."

"That's right, Boss. Barney can be bought."

Maybe, maybe not. Barnabas Soltairé was a man of mysterious motivations. His lifestyle reflected wealth and culture, but his decisions sometimes flew in the face of this desire for opulence. He'd closed down his law practice in order to manage this large family trust.

Serving on several boards, Soltairé was clearly a busy man. Nonetheless, he took Maddy's call without making her wait. A smart guy, he knew that when Miss Hilda passed away he'd be reporting directly to this newly discovered heir. Maddy was the dominant one of the twins, her sister Maisie preferring to remain on the sidelines.

"Madelyn Madison, to what do I owe the pleasure?" he greeted her with a practiced smoothness. He was a slick guy who could've convinced a jury that Jack Ruby's gun went off accidentally. And then get Lee Harvey Oswald to confirm that's what happened with his dying breath.

"Hello, Barnabas. I'm afraid I bring some disturbing news."

"Oh? What's the problem?"

"We've just uncovered four birth certificates that suggest the Hoople Quadruplets weren't really brother and sisters."

"Oh that. It's about time you were let in on what Miss Hilda calls the 'Family Secret.'"

"Are you saying you knew about this fraud?"

"Now now, Maddy. Don't call it a fraud. Think of it like professional wrestling – an entertainment. Everybody knows wrestling's not real, but nobody cares."

"That's a strange analogy."

"Best I could do on short notice," he chuckled. "You caught me off guard. I hadn't planned on telling you this until after Miss Hilda had passed."

"Are there any more secrets I should know about?"

"All in good time," he laughed. "One should drink a bottle of aged brandy one sip at a time."

"What should we do about these birth certificates?"

"Put them back in the safe with the adoption papers."

"Adoption papers? There were no adoption papers in that safe in the basement."

"They're around somewhere. Find them and you will have Secret Number Two."

"Secret Number Two? How many secrets are there?"

"Quite a few."

"Barnabas –!" she responded, but he had already hung up on her.

~ ~ ~

Secret Number Two? Barnabas Soltairé had confirmed that there was more to be discovered about the Hoople family.

Maddy couldn't help but be intrigued. Through no fault of her own, her life had been upended, landing her in the middle of this weird family who had lived in the spooky old mansion atop Hoople Hill.

Most of her life she had been confident that she was Madelyn Agnes Taylor, a descendant of the original settlers of Caruthers Corners. Then she had been told she was a Hoople. Now the cat was out of the bag, that her father wasn't really a Hoople. Goodness knows what her lineage might turn out to be!

But if Secret Number One was the fact that the Hoople Quadruplets were not actually quadruplets – not even biological brother and sisters – what could Secret Number Two be?

Soltairé had said she needed to find the adoption papers to get the answer to that. So it had something to do with the adoptions.

But what?

The only way to find out was to turn up those missing papers. Was that what the note in the box meant? SECRET PAPERS IN VAULT, it had said. Was that a hint as to where to find the adoption papers?

This called for another search of the Hoople Mansion.

Chapter Thirteen

Teddy D

Teddy D's dad didn't hesitate telling Deputy Truehart where to find him. The boy was down in Pitsville hanging out with his girlfriend. "Kick his butt for me," Big Al told the deputy. Apparently there wasn't much father-son bonhomie within the DiMacchio family.

The boy was not happy to see the police show up. But he didn't resist riding back to Caruthers Corners to be questioned by the police chief. He realized that refusal would likely lead to arrest. He knew Tommy Truehart had never liked him.

There was no interview room in the cramped concrete building that housed the Caruthers Corners Police Department, so they borrowed the conference room at the Town Hall. Located on the second floor of the red-brick building, the spartan room held a long mahogany table, a dozen hardback chairs and not much more. A small side table accommodated a metal water pitcher and plastic glasses. The only picture on the wall was a panoramic aerial view of the town as in appeared in the 1940s. A calendar advertised Buddy Flynn's Texaco. In the center of the table sat one of those conference phones that look like a squat miniature space ship.

"I didn't do nothing wrong," sniveled the boy. "Why're

you picking on me?"

Chief Purdue ignored him, pretending to study the notes on his clipboard. Finally, he looked up and asked, "Where were you on the night Boyd Aitkens got killed?"

Teddy D squirmed. "I don't remember."

"Think hard, Teddy. We have proof that you were within blocks of that meth lab after it blew up."

"Maybe I was. I do recall that I drove through town that night. Cruising, you know."

"No, Teddy, I don't. What do you mean by 'cruising'?"

"Just riding around. Seeing what's going on."

"Did you stop at Mr. Harribald apartment?"

"Who?"

"Don't play cute with me, Teddy. We know you know Justin Harribald." Jim Purdue was bluffing on that one. He had no connection between the two at all. Just the surveillance video that placed the boy's car three blocks away."

Teddy D bit. "Okay, so I know Mr. Harribald. That don't prove I blew up his place. Heck, he wasn't even home at the time of the explosion."

"How do you know that?"

"I read it in the *Burpyville Gazette*."

"Are you sure you didn't give Boyd Aitkens a lift, dropped him off at Harribald's apartment?" Jim was going on a hunch. Boyd Aikens' car wasn't found near the meth lab. How did he get there?

"So what if I gave Mr. Aitkens a ride? That ain't against the law."

"Why would you be playing chauffeur for a man like Boyd Aikens?"

"He was gonna give me a job. Maybe overseeing a watermelon pickin' crew, something like that. So I was helping him out.'"

"You don't impress me as the farmer type," challenged the police chief. "Why would you want a job out in the hot sun working with a bunch of Mexican melon pickers for $11.05 an hour?"

"It's better'n the $9.70 they pay at Walmart over in Burpyville."

"So you were going into the watermelon business?"

The boy was sweating profusely, despite the moderate temperature in the room. "Hey, I needed a job. I dropped outta school, and my old man kicked me outta the house. I been staying with my girlfriend down in Pitsville."

"Why were you in Pitsville if you're going to be working for Aitkens Produce?"

"When the news came that Mr. Aikens was dead, I figured that was the end of the job possibility."

"Did you ask his son Ralph Aitkens about the job? He's still foreman."

"I heard about that girl stealing the company out from under poor Ralph. I figured he didn't have no more say-so."

"Do you plan to stay down in Pitsville?"

"I'm back and forth. I got my pick-ups to make."

"Pick-ups?"

"Uh, never mind. I didn't mean to say that."

"What pick-ups?"

"I do deliveries sometimes. Make pick-ups and drop-offs."

"For whom?"

"That's all I'm saying. Either arrest me or let me go."

Chief Purdue had nothing to hold him on, short of declaring him a material witness. So he said, "Okay, you're free to go. But don't leave the county."

"Is Pitsville in the county?"

"Yes, it's in Caruthers County. Haven't you ever looked at a road map?"

"Not lately," said the surly teen. "Is Tommy gonna give me a ride back to Pitsville? That's where my wheels are."

"That's your problem," said Chief Purdue, signaling that the interview was over. "Get there best way you can."

~ ~ ~

Meanwhile, Lizzie Ridenour had hired Bob "Flash" Dougan to photograph the Frank Leslie Quilt. She needed something for the records, as well as a photo to send to the Indiana Museum of Art. She wanted to have the antique quilt authenticated by experts. She was impressed by the quilt collection at IMA.

Flash Dougan normally worked at the E-Z Seat factory photographing new chair styles for the sales catalogs. But he'd been out of work since that twister took off half the factory building. Thanks to the owner's generosity, he was still drawing a paycheck. But not working was boring. He was more than happy to pick up a few freelance jobs on the side whenever he could.

Flash had a makeshift studio in his garage. To photograph the quilt he used a wooden stepladder. That gave him enough height to capture the entirety of the textile's 102" x 91 ¾" surface. He adjusted hot floodlights on stands to get the lighting just right. Lizzie found it ironic that despite his nickname he didn't use a flash.

He focused carefully to make sure the image was sharp

from edge to edge. The quilt looked good in his viewfinder: 15 appliqués that alternated with quilted dove designs on a peach-colored satin backdrop.

Lizzie studied the quilt as he worked. In one corner was a discrete date: 1925. Another section was marked with a faint brown stain – the spilled chocolate, Lizzie assumed. The border was plain and unmarked.

Click! Click! Click! Flash Dougan captured a series of digital images of the entire quilt, then he moved in close to get shots of each individual appliqué – *Click! Click! Click!* – from the face of a female Santa to the portrait of a famous lighthouse keeper.

He only charged $50 for his time.

Chapter Fourteen

The Father-Son Reunion

"Mr. Harribald, meet your son Ralph," said Chief Jim Purdue.

The prisoner looked up as if his head were on a spring. "Ralph – is that you?"

Ralph Aitkens shuffled his feet, shifting his weight from one to another. "Mr. Harribald, I'm told you're my real father. Is that true?"

"Well, yes, I guess it is. Now that your dad – Boyd, that is – is dead, I suppose it's all right to admit it."

"Why couldn't you admit it before now?" Ralph looked confused.

"Because I signed a non-disclosure agreement. Boyd insisted on it. Otherwise, he threatened to get me fired from the high school. That was – how old are you? – thirtysome years ago."

"So you and my mom –?"

"June Johnson was one of my prize students. She made an A+ in my history class."

"My mom was in high school at the time?"

"That's right. But she dropped out of school when she found out you were on the way. Boyd – he was five or six years older than your mom – married her just before you were born. 'Nick of time,' he used to say."

"He was friendly with you?"

"Why not? He didn't even know your mom when she was in my class. They met right after she dropped out of school to have the baby – you, that is."

Ralph frowned. "Then why did you kill him?"

"I didn't. I was shopping for groceries at Food Lion when he blew himself up. I'd told him never to touch my methamphetamine set-up. Danged fool, never listened."

"I know that's true. My dad – Boyd, that is – was pretty hard headed. Went where he wanted, touched what he wanted, did what he wanted."

"Just because Boyd was my financial backer didn't give him the right to march into my apartment unannounced. Serves him right, getting blown to Kingdom Come. Oh, sorry, I didn't mean that."

~ ~ ~

Chief Purdue took this exchange between Ralph Aitkens and his biological father with a grain of salt. They were saying the right things, but somehow it struck him as disingenuous, like they were speaking predetermined lines, like characters in a stage play.

Were they putting on a performance for his benefit? Or was this a genuine first-time reunion of father and son?

It was pretty obvious that Boyd Aitkens's death was accidental. But there was something else going on here. As if a crime was being committed under his very nose ... and he didn't know what it was.

~ ~ ~

"Mr. Harribald, are you ready to make a statement?" asked Chief Purdue. The elderly man had refused to comment on the situation so far. But after meeting his son, he seemed ready to talk. "Unless you clear things up, I'm going to have to charge you under Indiana Code Section 35-48-4-1 et seq. That's 'a person who knowingly or intentionally manufactures; finances the manufacture of; delivers; or finances the delivery of illicit drugs ... or possesses, with intent to do any of the above.' "

"You're accusing me of financing the manufacture of drugs – ha! If I had the money to do that, I wouldn't have needed Boyd."

"I'll also have to charge you under Indiana Code Section 35-42-1-4. That's involuntary manslaughter, an 'unintentional killing that results from recklessness or criminal negligence, or from an unlawful act that is a misdemeanor or low-level felony' – like manufacturing meth."

"How much time am I looking at? I'm 76 now. I'd hate to spend the rest of my life in prison."

"Depends. I'm no lawyer. But it'll go lighter if you cooperate. How about making a statement. You haven't said a word since we brought you in."

"That's because I don't have a lawyer. I'm not going to spill my guts without a lawyer."

"Want a court-appointed attorney? That can be arranged."

"Sure. Why not? I don't have any money to pay a lawyer. If I did, I wouldn't be cooking meth on the side."

Enter J. Harold Wentworth. Like a bad penny.

~ ~ ~

Johnny Wentworth was going for the gold, knowing he wouldn't be practicing law much longer. His uncle – The Honorable John Lawrence Bristol – might be able to keep him out of jail on those charges of dipping into escrow funds, but the judge's reach didn't extend to the State Bar. "Bust-'em-Out" Bristol had made too many enemies there. So Johnny was taking any last-minute cases he could haul in before being disbarred.

Representing Ralph Aitkens was a "gimme," being that Johnny had done a lot of legal work for Ralph's father. Boyd had used him for a number of real estate deals, a parcel-by-parcel land grab that had made him into a watermelon baron.

Justin Harribald was a referral, the bill being footed by Aitkens Produce.

"We don't want him to talk," Ralph had said to Wentworth. "Too risky."

Luckily, this should be a quick *habeas corpus* job, faster the better, because the new owner of the watermelon farm might not be inclined to pay his bill. He sure hadn't seen Suzy Aitkens coming. Obviously, ol' Boyd played his cards close to the vest. His boy Ralph had been blindsided too. Nobody knew of this secret love child from Pitsville.

Johnny wasn't sure whether Ralph was picking up the tab on Justin Harribald because the old man had been his dad's partner in the meth lab ... or because he'd been revealed to be Ralph's true daddy.

No matter, a client was a client. He'd already arranged with his uncle to issue the Writ of Habeas Corpus. It was a done deal.

The local police chief – a hick named Jim Purdue – would blow a gasket. He'd already pulled this *habeas corpus* routine on him a few months ago with a crook calling himself Robert di Nero. Like the famous actor. He'd had di Nero out of jail before the police chief got the cell door locked.

Johnny hadn't been sure his uncle would do it again, but Ralph had come up with prerequisite $25,000 – $10,000 for Johnny and $15,000 for the judge. Happened that Bust-'em-Out Bristol had just dropped a bundle in the weekly poker game with the Burpyville mayor, so he jumped at it.

$15 grand was $15 grand.

Chapter Fifteen

Rev. Dimpledorf

"Rev. David Dimpledorf," said Maddy as she spread the four birth certificates across the Formica tabletop like a deck of playing cards. "That's the common denominator on all these documents."

Another rainy day, the Quilters Club had gathered in their regular corner booth at Cozy Café. The stainless-steel-fronted diner lived up to its name on a day like this – cozy.

Aggie had tagged along, her school closed again because of its leaky roof. N'yen chose to go over to the Haney Bros. Zoo and Exotic Animal Refuge to help his Uncle Ben wash Happy the Elephant. In the middle of a heavy rain was a good time to scrub down a dusty pachyderm. Wasn't like he could fit in a bath tub.

Maisie Walters handed out porcelain cups of "Good to the Last Drop" Maxwell House coffee, also delivering a tall glass of watermelon-flavored milk for Aggie. Then she pulled up a chair and joined them. As a Hoople heir, she had a stake in this new discovery about the famous quadruplets.

"Dimpledorf – I recognize that name," said Maisie. "He's the guy who handled my and Maddy's adoption."

Lizzie nodded. "Yes, he was that TV evangelist who got shot by one of his parishioners. We looked into his organization back when we first found out you guys were adopted."

"Rev. Dimple – as he was called – was selling off babies to the highest bidder," said Maddy. "Looks like he'd been at it for years."

"You're saying he did the same thing with your Aunt Hilda and her siblings?" asked Bootsie, looking at the birth certificates on the table.

"No, just the opposite," explained Maddy. "Here he didn't split up twins. He took four orphans and passed them off as quadruplets."

"You mean the Hoople Quadruples aren't real?" gasped Cookie. Genealogy charts shifting in her head.

"Not according to these birth certificates that Aggie found in a safe in the basement," said Maddy, sipping at her coffee. Cozy Café still had the best java in town.

"Does that mean Aunt Hilda isn't really our aunt?" asked Maisie, a quaver in her voice. She was just getting used to being part of the Hoople family.

"Not biologically," said Maddy, her round face looking very sad. "Hilda and our father – Howard Hoople – weren't actually related. All four of the so-called quadruplets were adopted, each from a different family."

"But that's impossible," Bootsie shook her head, ruffling her pixie-length hair with the exertion. "An adoption agency couldn't get away with passing off four separate babies as quads."

"That was in the '30s. Things were loosey goosey back then."

Lizzie looked confused. "These papers say Caring Home for Unwed Mothers. I thought Rev. Dimple's organization was the Forever Family Foundation."

"Maybe he changed its name."

"Yeah, maybe –"

"Ladies, hold up right there," interjected Cookie. "You can forget this implausible theory."

"What do you mean 'implausible'?" said Lizzie. Insulted by the aspersion.

"The numbers don't add up." As executive director of the Caruthers Corners Historical Society, she had a heightened awareness of dates. She could calculate years and calendar dates with the precision of an *idiot savant*.

"– don't add up?"

"Do the math for yourself. Rev. Dimpledorf was 88 when he died two years ago. I remember the obituary. That would have made him five-years-old when Hilda and the three others were placed with Henry and Henrietta Hoople. I think five's a little young to be running a home for unwed mothers – no matter what you call it."

"But his name is on these birth certificates," Maddy pointed out. "Here, look at the stamp. And there's his pen-and-ink signature. Quite a squiggle, but you can make out the D-I-M-P."

"Numbers don't lie," insisted the blonde historian. "These birth certificates must be bogus."

"Sounds like somebody's playing a dirty trick on the Hoople family," agreed Bootsie. Easily swayed.

"If the birth certificates are fake, that might mean the quadruplets are brother and sisters after all," said Cookie, the genealogy charts rearranging themselves inside her head once again.

"Whew!" sighed Maisie, as if putting aside a bad dream. "I was worried there for a minute."

"Hold on – don't be so quick," cautioned Maddy. "If the birth certificates are fake, why did Aunt Hilda confess to the charade?"

"She's getting old and confused," suggested Lizzie. "The Parkinson's."

"Yes, but Barnabas Soltairé also confirmed it," Maddy pointed out. "I spoke with him only yesterday."

"Well, that's hard to refute," acquiesced Lizzie.

"What about the age discrepancy?" persisted Cookie. "Rev. Dimpledorf can't be five-years-old and signing birth certificates at the same time."

"Right," agreed Bootsie. "Both things can't be true."

"Maybe they can," said Aggie, a new thought popping into her head.

"How so?" Cookie wanted to know. You could always count on 1 + 1 = 2 in her orderly worldview.

"What if there were *two* Rev. Dimpledorfs?"

"Two?"

"Yes," nodded Aggie. "Father and son."

Chapter Sixteen

Domestic Disturbance

Deputy Pete Hitzer got a call from the dispatcher asking him to check out a domestic disturbance up in Crackleton Crossing. The little community was an enclave of – to use Hilary Clinton's word – deplorables.

"They're lower class, lower income, and lower intelligence nutjobs," asserted Fat Karl Schaeffer. He lived nearby, a fact that didn't help the value of his two-story farmhouse. His wife had inherited the 20-acre plot from her parents. Fat Karl hadn't been able to sell the house due to its proximity to the Crossing.

Crackletons were all but pariahs in these parts.

Petie disliked calls to Crackleton Crossing. It was a dangerous place for a lone policeman. High unemployment and alcoholism produced a populace that milled about as aimlessly as zombies in *Day of the Dead*. Violence rippled beneath the surface.

The close-knit community was ruled by 99-year-old Granny Crackleton, the matriarch who gave the crossroads its name. There were no businesses here, other than her son's overpriced convenience store, a sewing notions shop, and a windows-barred gun store. The convenience store sold a lot of beer.

Coors Light and Pabst Blue Ribbon were good sellers.

But craft beer from 3 Floyds led the pack – stouts and ales like Alpha King, Zombie Dust, Permanent Funeral, Wigsplitter, and Bourbon Barrel Aged Vanilla Bean Dark Lord. Also scoring high on the list was 18th Street Brewery's Bitches' Bank, Crack the Skye, and Deal With the Devil.

Since the Crackletons' Jiffy Mart was lax about checking IDs, there was quite a bit of underage drinking hereabouts.

Petie parked his cruiser in front of the address Myrtle Dobbler had given him, a small clapboard house with peeling white paint. The rust on the tin roof was as dark as dried blood. Stepping out of the CCPD Dodge Charger, he proceeded to the front door and pounded on it with his billy club. "Police," he called.

Although Crackleton Crossing was outside the town limits, the Caruthers Corners Police Department had the authority to patrol the entire county. Due to money-saving consolidations back in the late '50s there was no sheriff's department.

"Go away," came a voice.

"We got a call about a situation. Husband and wife altercation."

The door swung open to reveal a woman with a black eye. It was swollen shut, like a prize fighter before the cut. "We ain't married," she said. Defiance in her voice.

Petie Hitzer knew few people bothered with marriage in Crackleton Crossing. Baby Daddies came and went. Everybody was related to everybody up here. "Who hit you?" he asked.

"Don't know his name."

"Has this this man been living here with you?"

"For about a month now."

"And you don't know his name?"

"I forgot to ask."

"What's your name?"

"Faith Ann Ritchie."

The deputy gave her a closer look. "You're Granny Crackleton's daughter, aren't you?"

"That's right. What of it?"

"That makes you Gus's mama, the kid Ben and Cookie Bentley are fostering."

She shrugged. "He's one of mine, the little snotnose. Glad to have him off my back. His daddy don't pay no support."

"Who is his daddy?"

"Don't remember off the top of my head. I'm sure it's on his birth certificate."

Chapter Seventeen

History Lesson

The Caruthers Corners Historical Society took up an entire wing of the Perricock Museum of Science & History, the big stone edifice that sat on the adjacent hillside to the Hoople Mansion. Cookie Bentley had served as its executive director for the past twenty years or so.

After the morning's gathering at Cozy Café, Cookie hurried over to the Historical Society to search the files, looking for any references to a Rev. David Dimpledorf. She wanted to check out Aggie's "Two Dimpledorfs" theory. It would satisfy her questions about the age discrepancy.

Plowing through the yellowing folders, she found plenty of mentions of Forever Family Foundation and the famous televangelist known as Rev. Dimple.

An unconvicted pedophile, Rev. Dimple took advantage of the young female adoptees – "Dimple's Darlings," he called them. Later, one of the victims shot him dead. The Quilters Club had led the behind-the-scenes charge to get Forever Family Foundation closed down.

However, there was nothing in the Society's files about a father or the Caring Home For Unwed Mothers.

A historical blind spot?

~ ~ ~

After Nightly Newspapers bought the *Burpyville*

Gazette, the new owner sold off the paper's back-issue microfiche to Caruthers Corner Historical Society. Maddy's trust fund helped the Historical Society acquire the spools of microfiche along with a new reader. So next Cookie went into her "microfiche room" (a former pantry) and fired up the machine. Pulling out the spools of film for the 1920s and 1930s, she continued her search. Nothing. So she pulled out 1940s and 1950s. That's when she began to pick up a few squibs about the son – a television evangelist known to his viewers as Rev. Dimple.

But she was looking for the father.

The *Burpyville Gazette* had no mention.

~ ~ ~

The Indiana Historical Society likes to call itself "Indiana's Storyteller." Located in the Eugene and Marilyn Glick Indiana History Center on the Canal in downtown Indianapolis, its Collections Department offers one of the largest archival repositories of manuscript, printed and visual materials on the history of Indiana. This includes 70,000 online digital images, 5,450 processed manuscripts, 1,700 maps, 1.7 million photographs, 3,300 artifacts, and 129 paintings. Among its primary collecting areas is the topic of religion.

Cookie placed a call to a friend at the Society to ask about the first Rev. David Dimpledorf.

"We don't have much on him," she was told. "He was some kind of faith healer. Involved in family charities. Sorry, but we don't have anything more than that."

"Where can I go to find out about Rev. David Dimpledorf's Caring Home For Unwed Mothers?"

"Hard to say. I'm not sure I've ever heard of it."

"Surely there's someone I can talk with."

"Hmmm. There's an old-timer at IU who might be able to help you out. A professor by the name of Angus Middleton. He's familiar with all the old Bible-thumpers. Middleton wrote a book on the religious history of Indianapolis."

"A thin book, I'd guess." A joke. Ha! Ha!

"Actually, it's a pretty thick tome," her friend corrected her. "The city is the seat of the Roman Catholic Archdiocese of Indianapolis. Also the Episcopal Diocese of Indianapolis, the Indiana-Kentucky Synod of the Evangelical Lutheran Church in America, and the Indiana Conference of the United Methodist Church – they're all based here. Indy has a lot of religious history."

"I stand corrected," said Cookie.

"Don't apologize. While there may be a vast religious history in Indianapolis, surveys show that nearly 60 per cent of the city's residents identify themselves as being non-religious."

~ ~ ~

She caught Dr. Angus Middleton between classes at Indiana University. With a Ph.D. in religious studies, he had written a well-regarded tome called *The Circle of Faith in Circle City*. He required his students to buy the textbook, even though his two classes were Medieval Religious Theory and Spirited Spirituality.

"Yes, I wrote a book on religion in Indianapolis," he confirmed, sounding in a hurry to get to a class. "What can I tell you, Mrs. Bentley?"

"I'm trying to find out about a turn-of-the-century evangelist named David Arthur Dimpledorf."

"Oh, that old humbug." His voice sounded far away over the phone. "He was the father of Rev. Dimple, founder of the Forever Home Foundation. The son was much more famous. Got shot in a sex scandal, you probably know."

"Yes, but about the father –?"

"Rev. Dimple's father came to Indianapolis in the early '20s as a traveling revivalist. Did tent shows. A healer who claimed to cure afflictions of body and mind – for a donation, of course. Nobody gave him much heed till he started up a home for unwed mothers."

"What motivated him to do that?"

"This is just conjecture, of course, but it was said he started it when he got one of his parishioners pregnant. David Jr.'s mom, the rumor had it."

"Rev. Dingle was illegitimate?"

"Well, he was conceived out of wedlock. It was never clear whether Rev. Dimpledorf married the mother or not. Records are sketchy."

"Can you tell me anything about this Caring Home for Unwed Mothers?"

"Not much. That's out of my purview. But it was like that old Steve Martin joke about supporting a home for unwed mothers because he gave so many of the girls their start."

"So the old man was a womanizer?"

"Big time. It wasn't exactly the spirit of the Lord entering his female followers, if you know what I mean. Later on, the son was just as bad – a family tradition of philandering."

"Doesn't sound like you think very highly of the Dimpledorfs."

"They were religious charlatans. A stain on the city's fine religious history. An embarrassment to true Christian ministries."

"So the Caring Home for Unwed Mothers wasn't on the up-and-up?"

"Word was it was a baby black market, selling off unwanted children to the highest bidder. It's a wonder the old crook didn't go to prison. Same is true for Dimple Jr."

"You're sure about this?"

"I've extensively researched my book on Indianapolis's religious history. From the 1821 classes held by Methodist in a log cabin on West Washington to the 1823 Presbyterian meetings on Market Street to the 1928 Baptist church at the southwest corner of Monument Circle and Meridian – it's all there in *The Circle of Faith in Circle City*."

"Impressive."

"The oldest religious group in Indiana is, of course, the Roman Catholic Church. It was established around 1750 by the French at Vincennes. In 1837 Saint John the Evangelist Catholic Church began serving Holy Cross parish in Indianapolis. Then, in 1898, Pope Leo XIII transferred the episcopal see from Vincennes to Indianapolis. Now Roman Catholics account for the largest religious group in the city."

"What about Rev. Dimpledorf's church?"

"The evangelists came much later on. In the early 1900s Billy Sunday was a frequent speaker at gospel revivals in Indianapolis. An Elmer Gantry character like Rev. David Dimpledorf was inevitable back in the '20s."

"Can you tell me anything more about the Caring Home for Unwed Mothers?"

"The Home went out of business in the '30s. It's not

clear why."

"Thank you for your insights," replied Cookie, recording these details in her eidetic memory bank. "The Dimpledorfs sound like bad apples."

"Rotten to the core," said the professor. "Now excuse me, I'm late for class."

~ ~ ~

Cookie realized that she needed to check back issues of the *Indianapolis Star*. After all, Indy had been the headquarters for the Dimpledorf ministry. The *Star*'s archives go all way back to 1869. Available through Newspapers.com, the Historical Society had a subscription ($7.95 a month) that gave Cookie access to the newspaper's computerized archives. She entered her password and began a fresh search.

The first mention of a Rev. David Dimpledorf turned up in the August 12, 1924, issue of the *Star*, a brief notation about "a tent revival at the fairgrounds." The announcement promised "healing, salvation, and miracles" – a "laying on of hands by Rev. Dimpledorf." Donations would be accepted.

The early '20s just like Professor Middleton had said.

The second mention she came across in the *Star*'s back issues heralded a major milestone for Rev. Dimpledorf's ministry:

INDIANAPOLIS, INDIANA – Rev. David Dimpledorf continues his good work with the establishment of a domicile for women facing unwanted or unintended pregnancies, the purpose being to place their babies with loving families. "The Caring Home for Unwed Mothers is at its heart an adoption agency," said the popular evangelical minister. "We don't want the little children to suffer for their mothers' sins." The new facility will be located on the east side of the city. The organization will serve both Indiana and Ohio families in its Christian adoption outreach.

The date of the article was May 12, 1928 – Mother's Day, as it turned out.

~ ~ ~

Mother's Day – always the second Sunday in May – was established as a national holiday in 1914 by the proclamation of President Woodrow Wilson. This was at the initiative of Ann Reeves Jarvis, a West Virginia peace activist who campaigned for a day to honor her late mother.

According to his official biography, Rev. David Arthur Dimpledorf, Jr. was born on that same Mother's Day in 1928. An interesting coincidence, Cookie thought. Maybe there was something to the IU professor's claim that the Caring Home for Unwed Mothers was founded to handle a parishioner impregnated by the Rev. Dimpledorf.

Little was known about Rev. Dimple's father. Coverage of him between the early '20s and his death in 1950 due to a heart attack was thin. There was little information on his adoption practices.

According to the newspaper reports, the son took over the ministry in the early '50s, setting up a non-profit called Forever Family Foundation. There was a twenty year gap between FFF and the Caring Home For Unwed Mothers. The recycling of an earlier idea? Was it a ministry or an adoption scam?

Chapter Eighteen

The Caring Home for Unwed Mothers

Having come up with the "Two Dimpledorfs" theory, Aggie decided to do a little research on her own. Her natural inclination would have been to go down to the town library. Miss Mary Hegler had been the librarian there for as long as anyone could remember. She'd been one of Aggie's mentors, encouraging the girl's love of books. But now Miss Hegler was like a queen without a kingdom. The library had been totally destroyed by the recent tornado. All the books ripped apart and turned into scrap paper by the cyclonic winds. Only a concrete slab indicated the spot where the Caruthers Corners Public Library had once stood.

Bummer.

That meant she had to turn to N'yen. As much as she hated to ask a favor of her cantankerous cousin, she had no choice. The little nerd had written his own search engine program, one that sent "spiders" into cyberspace, searching in nooks and crannies where Google never ventured. He had been offered a six-figure price for it by a big Silicon Valley company, but he was holding out for more.

"Say please," he named his price for the favor.

"Pretty please with toadstools on it," Aggie replied.

Not exactly what he was looking for, but close enough. "Okay, you're trying to find any references to a Rev. David

Dimpledorf – senior, not junior?"

"That's right. Turn of the century to the '30s, I'd guess."

"That might be hard," he warned in advance. "The World Wide Web didn't exist back then. Lots of things have never been digitized."

"Give it a try," she coaxed. "You're the guy with the super-duper browser."

"Search engine," he corrected. "A browser is a software program that provides access to the Internet. A search engine is a program that can search the Internet for an entered keyword and find any matching documents or web pages."

"Thank you, Bill Nye the Science Guy."

"I consider that a compliment," sniffed the Asian boy. "He's one of my heroes."

"Probably you idolize Professor Proton too," she referred to a fictional character played by Bob Newhart on *The Big Bang Theory*.

"Do you want me to help you or had you rather keep trying to insult me, Miss Nancy Drew."

"I consider that a compliment," she said in return. "But let's do the search. I'm trying to help Grammy here."

"Roger dodger," he responded obediently and began clicking the keyboard on his computer. It was a Dell Precision 7730, one of the most powerful mobile workstations in the world. With its Intel Core Xeon E-2186M 6-Core CPU, Nvidia Quadro P5200 16GB GPU, ECC - 64GB DDR4 2,400MHz RAM, Non-ECC - 32GB DDR4 2,666MHz RAM, and 2TB M.2 NVMe PCIe SSD (x4), it was priced at $11,500. Fortunately, N'yen had secured a grant to buy it. He was getting pretty good at grant writing.

N'yen's search engine could go where others couldn't – into corporate records and governmental databases, even the Dark Web. Despite its prowess, the search engine didn't turn up much – just a few stray references – about a 1920s tent revivalist by the name of David Dimpledorf.

By contrast, there was a ton of information about his son, the notorious Rev. Dimple. Mostly lurid accounts of the minister's carryings-on with his flock, accusations of financial maleficence, and reports of his death, shot between the eyes with a .22 Saturday Night Special by a former Dimple's Darling named Betty Binkweather.

It looked like a dead end. Literally.

Bummer.

"Have you checked birth records?" asked N'yen.

"No. I didn't think of that," Aggie admitted.

"Here goes." The boy began to tap on his keyboard.

He quickly accessed The Indiana Division of Vital Records, hacking around VitalChek, an expedited service that requires a fee. He scrolled down the screen page. *A*s, *B*s, *C*s, coming to *D*s.

Success! He located a birth certificate dated May 12, 1928, for one David Arthur Dimpledorf, Jr. Parents listed as David Arthur Dimpledorf and Mary Jo Patterson.

"There *was* a father!" she exclaimed.

N'yen rolled his eyes, the gesture nearly hidden behind the epicanthic fold of his eyelids. "There's always a father," he said. "Don't you know anything about sex?"

"More than you think, Mr. Smarty Pants."

"Yeah, I've seen you practicing down there in the cemetery."

"What! – you've been spying on me, you little perv?"

"The mating habits of the local citizenry is not all that interesting to me," he dismissed her indignation.

~ ~ ~

"Now that we've proved there were two Dimpledorf's, let's see what can we find about the Caring Home for Unwed Mothers. Was that a different organization from the Forever Families Foundation?"

"Give me a sec." He tapped at the keyboard.

A few minutes later he reported: "I've got 2,012 hits for Forever Family Foundation, zero for Caring Home for Unwed Mothers."

"But it must have existed. We've got birth certificates to prove it."

"But those birth certificates were never registered." When he'd been inside the database for The Indiana Division of Vital Records, he'd looked for any records of the quadruplets. Nothing.

"Try variations on the name."

"I think my search engine would have picked that up."

"Try anyway."

"If you insist." His cousin could be quite bossy, but he was used to that.

Caring Home For Unwed Mothers.

Nothing again.

Unwed Home For Caring Mothers.

Nothing.

Unwed Mothers' Caring Home.

Ditto.

Caring Home For Mothers.

Bingo!

Tucked away in the FBI's database he located a scanned

copy of a 1934 investigation into the adoption practices of an Indianapolis organization simply identified as "Caring Home for Mothers."

According to the handwritten report by an FBI agent who signed his name as *Fogerty* or *Fogarty*:

> *"The evidence suggests this facility is a baby mill that sells infants to the highest bidder. But when records were subpoenaed, a fire destroyed the Home and all its records. There were no injuries, as all the women under its care had been taken on an unannounced 'field trip.' The fire department reported finding traces of accelerants. The manager of the Caring Home for Mothers attributed the fire to 'enemies of God.' He said the facility would not be reopening. Due to the fire it will be impossible to trace any 'adoptions' during the past decade of its operation as planned. The owner of the facility is identified as David Arthur Dimpledorf, a self-ordained minister in the Church of Eminent Salvation, a sect loosely affiliated with the Pentecostals. This case is being closed for lack of supporting evidence."*

"This proves it!" shouted Aggie. "The Hoople Quadruples were black market babies sold off by Rev. Dimple's father."

"This isn't proof. It merely states an FBI suspicion," corrected her cousin.

"It's good enough for me. Besides Rev. Dimpledorf's name was stamped all over those birth certificates. Now, if we could just find the adoption records. That might show the quad's real mothers and fathers."

"What's the big deal who their real parents were?" As an adoptee, N'yen found "parents" a relative, ever-changing term.

"Because Howard Hoople's birth mother would be my great, great grandmother. I'm curious who she was. And where I came from."

"Didn't your mother tell you a stork brought you?"

"I thought you said you weren't interested in the mating habits of local citizenry," she retorted.

That shut him up.

PART II

"It's mother!" cried Wendy, peeping.

"So it is!" said John.

"Then are you not really our mother, Wendy?" asked Michael, who was surely sleepy.

- Peter Pan, J.M. Barrie

Chapter Nineteen

Methamphetamine

Although it wasn't a Tuesday, the Quilters Club decided to reconvene. Working on their quilts was a handy excuse for catching up on the whirlwind of recent events.

First item on the agenda, Lizzie Ridenour wanted to complain about Justin Harribald running a meth lab across the street from the quilting museum. "That old fool could have blown us all up," huffed the feisty redhead. "How irresponsible!"

"And highly illegal," added Bootsie Purdue. Miss Law and Order. "He'll certainly do jail time. It's both a state and federal crime."

"How come we didn't know there was a meth lab across the street?" Maddy Madison raised the question. "I hear the manufacturing process creates foul odors that make such labs difficult to conceal."

"Not anymore," clarified N'yen, sounding as if he were an expert in cooking methamphetamine crystals. "There's a new method for making meth that doesn't smell as bad. I told you about it – Shake 'n Bake, it's called. Before that, labs were usually concealed in rural areas because of the smell, but now they can be located anywhere."

"How do you know about stuff this?" asked Bootsie suspiciously.

"Well –"

"I know," interjected his grandmother, "you read."

"Right," he nodded with a grin.

"I'm sorry, but I have trouble picturing Mr. Harribald as a drug kingpin," said Lizzie. All four of the women had been in his history classes back in high school. He's been a Lothario, to be sure, but no one had ever bought drugs from him. He'd seemed pretty harmless, if you stayed out of his octopus grasp.

"Yes," responded Cookie. "Drugs are certainly out of character for Justin. He didn't even smoke tobacco, much less use weed or hard stuff. He was a kind, decent man. A true intellectual."

"Of course, you'd say that," teased Bootsie. She enjoyed jerking her friend's chain. "But I doubt you and him were having study sessions."

"C'mon," replied the blonde. "My fling with Justin Harribald was ages ago. Now he's just a creepy old man."

~ ~ ~

"Anything new on the quad's parentage?" asked Lizzie, deliberately changing the subject. Cookie could be thin skinned when reminded of her youthful indiscretions – especially in front of Aggie and N'yen. Best to avoid pushing that button too hard.

"Aunt Hilda admits the quads knew about the deception from an early age, but went along with it," reported Maddy. She sorted her fabric pieces as she talked, still working on the Drunkard's Path quilt. It was trickier than she'd expected. "The Hoople family got rich. The children were treated like royalty. Everybody was in on it."

"That's kind of sad," said Bootsie. "The idea that your

Aunt Hilda spent her whole life living a lie."

"Rev. Dimple ruined a lot of lives with his questionable adoptions," Maddy declared. "Mine and Maisie's, the Hoople Quadruples, hundreds of others I'd guess."

"No, it wasn't just Rev. Dimple," said Cookie. "I did some research. Aggie was right. There were two Dimpledorfs. Father and son."

"Two? You're sure?"

"Yes – the Rev. Dimple who placed you with the Taylors was actually David Dimpledorf, Jr. According to back issues of the *Indianapolis Star*, his father was also named David Dimpledorf. And he was a minister too."

"That explains the age discrepancy," said Lizzie.

"No wonder we were confused," sighed Maddy. The pieces of the puzzle starting to fit together.

"N'yen and I did some research too," announced Aggie. "According to an old FBI report, the G-Men were going after the original Rev. Dimpledorf for running a baby mill, but the Caring Home for Unwed Mothers mysteriously burned down in 1934 along with all the records. So there's no telling how many adoptions they handled."

"Then his son opened a new operation in the '50s," said N'yen. "Carrying on the family business."

Aggie nodded. "The Forever Family Foundation – that's the one that placed you guys. The Caring Home for Unwed Mothers – that's the one that placed the quads."

"An FBI report?" said Bootsie. "How did you get your hands on that?"

"Don't ask," said Maddy. Eyeing her grandchildren sternly. She didn't approve of N'yen hacking into government databases. She was pretty sure that was illegal.

"But if the Hoople Quadruplets are fakes, what does that mean for the family trust fund?" asked Lizzie. The banker's wife, always thinking about money.

"Dunno," said Maddy. "That's a question I'll have to ask Mark the Shark."

"Why not ask Barnabas Soltairé? He's the Hoople Quadruplets Trust Fund's executive director."

"Because I'm not sure I can trust Barnabas. He's known about the deception all along."

Chapter Twenty

The Laundromat

Suzy Aitkens had spent the past several days signing legal documents related to the probate of her father's will. She got the farm, but voluntarily gave 49 per cent of it to Ralph, the brother she was not really related to. He was too depressed over discovering his true parentage to properly show his appreciation.

But Suzy was a smart cookie. She'd majored in Business Administration at Indiana Wesleyan University-Marion. This private university offered five degree programs in that field. Universities.com ranked it as first among the Best Business Administration and Management Colleges in Indiana.

All morning Suzy had laboriously gone over the books for Aitkens Produce. The company appeared to be profitable and well managed. Everything added up ... except for something identified as "Pharmaceutical Division." What the heck was that?

Louise Gluck, the head accountant, simply shrugged and said she had no idea, that she'd merely put down the numbers Boyd Aitkens had dictated. After all, it was his business.

Strange.

One notation she found said "methamphetamine."

What was that used for on a watermelon farm? Was it an enzyme that grew bigger melons? A pesticide? Or something else?

Suzy found a computer in the corner of the office and Googled the term.

Methamphetamine was the drug known on the street as meth. Crystal meth, she knew about. She had a girlfriend who'd been hooked on "poor man's cocaine."

She read:

> "Methamphetamine is a potent central nervous system (CNS) stimulant that's mainly used as a recreational drug.
>
> "The old meth labs required hundreds of pseudoephedrine pills, containers heated over open flames and cans of flammable liquids. Cooking, it was called.
>
> "But a new method of manufacturing – known as the 'one-pot' or 'shake and bake' method – requires only a few pseudoephedrine pills, circumventing laws that restricting the sale of large quantities of over-the-counter decongestants, cold and allergy remedies, the ingredients needed to make meth.
>
> "In this scenario meth is produced in a two-liter soda bottle. A few cold pills are mixed with common, but noxious, household chemicals, producing enough meth for the user to get a few hits.
>
> "But the shake and bake method is even more dangerous than the old makeshift meth labs, authorities say. If the bottle is shaken the wrong way, or if any oxygen gets inside of it, or if the cap is loosened too quickly, the bottle can explode.
>
> "If the old clandestine meth labs caught fire, the 'cooks' would just run away. But with the shake and bake method, they are actually holding the bottle when it

explodes. Police have linked dozens of flash fires — some of them fatal — to meth manufacturing.

"After years of declining numbers of meth labs being busted by law enforcement, due to the laws restricting the sale of pseudoephedrine, seizures are suddenly increasing again."

"Holy Jesus in a gin mill," gulped Suzy Aitkens. "My dad owned that meth lab that killed him in its explosion." Why else would he have been co-mingling "methamphetamine" profits into his watermelon business?

Laundering money.

Chapter Twenty-One

Not an Intervention

When Mark Tidemore got home from the Mayor's Office at 7:34 that night, he found the Quilters Club waiting for him in the parlor. Everybody had already had supper; that is, everybody except for him. And he could see that wasn't going to happen anytime soon. The four women and two teenagers looked determined to talk with him before he made another step toward the dining room.

"What is this?" he asked. "An intervention? Did my wife put you gals up to this? I know I've been spending too many hours at the Town Hall. But recovering from a tornado is a big task."

"No, no. It's not that," said his mother-in-law. "It's just that we have an important legal question to ask you."

Mark Tidemore smiled. His pearly white teeth were one of his better features. He was a handsome man in a Dylan McDermott kind of way. "C'mon, you know I'm no longer a lawyer. Gave it up to cut my salary by half as the town's mayor."

"Hmm, you may be right," jibed Lizzie Ridenour. "You may be too stupid to answer our question."

"Okay," he gave in. "What question?"

"Well, it's like this," began Maddy. "The Hoople Quadruplets are phony."

"W-what?" The quads were a major part of the town's heritage. Caruthers Corners used to promote itself as HOME OF THE HOOPLE QUADRUPLES. People even came from other states to visit this out-of-the-way burg just to say they'd been to the quadruplets' hometown.

Mark Tidemore raised his eyebrows, unable to hide his surprise. "You're saying the Hoople Quadruples were some kind of fraud?"

"I'm afraid so. Your daughter Aggie found the proof. Their birth certificates. Although the documents only refer to them as Girl 1, Girl 2, Girl 3, and Boy 1."

"Boy what?"

"Pay attention," instructed Maddy. "

Then she laid it all out for him – the Hoople family's con game.

He was still trying to get used to this. "You're saying they weren't even brothers and sisters?"

"Nope, all were adopted from different families through an organization called Rev. David Dimpledorf's Caring Home For Unwed Mothers."

"Rev. Dimpledorf? Wasn't he a TV minister? Shot by one of his followers?"

"That was the son. He ran the Forever Family Foundation, the organization that adopted out me and my twin sister Maisie."

"And the father?"

"The fruit doesn't fall far from the tree, as the saying goes. The father made illegal adoptions too – through his Caring Home for Unwed Mothers. Aggie and N'yen traced it down. The FBI called it a baby mill."

"That's a pretty serious charge."

"But true. Henry and Henrietta Hoople were big supporters, according to records we found in an old safe downstairs. Rev. David Dimpledorf's Caring Home for Unwed Mothers – that's where the four 'quadruplets' came from. Each child from a different family."

"Wow!"

Maddy smiled. "So does this mean I'm double illegitimate – the bastard daughter of a bastard son?" She found the idea amusing.

Her son-in-law patted her hand. "I wouldn't worry too much about that, mom. People take you for who you are."

"You mean an aging busybody who solves crimes?"

"That ... and the mother of three great children."

"I suppose that *is* some degree of accomplishment," she acquiesced.

"And don't forget seven great grandchildren," Aggie interjected. A little self-promotion there.

Maddy wasn't through with her questioning. "Tell me, Mark. Do I have to give the trust fund back? Fruit of the poisoned tree, or whatever you lawyers call it?"

"That has a different legal meaning," he assured her. "But to answer your question, you get to keep the money. The Hoople Quadruplets Trust Fund had the legal right to award it to you and your sister Maisie."

"Even if the Hoople Quadruples acquired that money under fraudulent circumstances?"

"There might be individual fraud charges against the family members, but all of the participants are dead – other than Aunt Hilda. Most of those claims would go back 60 or 70 years to when they were being paid for endorsements and public appearances. Probably most of those claimants are dead too."

"Is there a statute of limitations?"

"Maybe in some cases. But I think the defense would be that claimants got the publicity they were paying for – just as if they were hiring movie stars known for their on-screen roles."

"Like William Boyd making public appearances as Hopalong Cassidy?"

He laughed. "I had a more modern example in mind. Like William Shatner appearing at a Trekkie convention as Captain Kirk."

"That's not modern. Chris Pine plays Captain Kirk in today's movies."

"Sorry, Tilly and I don't see many *Star Wars* movies."

"You mean *Star Trek*."

"Those too."

"What about Aunt Hilda leaving us the mansion? Is that still possible? Or are we going to be homeless again?"

"Don't worry. Hilda was legally adopted by Henry and Henrietta Hoople, so that makes her an heir. As the last surviving family member, this old pile of rocks is hers to do with as she likes – leave it to you or turn it into a caring home for unwed mothers."

"There's more I want to know about this big quadruplet scam. We've got the birth certificates. But I think we need to find the adoption papers."

"A good idea. Now can I have my dinner?"

Chapter Twenty-Two

Maisie's Misgivings

"You have a visitor, madam," announced Marybelle Oliver.

Maddy was still getting used to having a "servant." Beau had taken to it like someone "to the manner born." Tilly too. Didn't fairytale castles come fully staffed?

Aggie and N'yen simply looked upon Marybelle as having their very own Mary Poppins – BBC accent and all.

"Who is it?" asked Maddy.

"Your sister Margaret."

"Oh. Show her in."

The British woman returned with Maisie Walters, then left to fetch tea. Tea was the answer to everything in the Hoople Mansion these days.

"Hi sis," she greeted Maddy. "This is the first time I've ever been in this big stone mausoleum."

"Really? Want a tour? After all, this is figuratively the family home."

"No thanks. That would take all day judging by the size of it. I've got to get back to work. The breakfast rush is over, but the waitress I left in charge hasn't had much experience. Still a trainee. Doesn't even know which side of the plate to put the utensils on."

"Relax and join me for some tea. I'm sure your new girl

will hold down the fort."

"This place is even bigger than it looks from the outside," observed Maisie, looking around the big room. A parlor, but it was the size of some small houses.

"Maisie, I have to ask. Are you okay with Aunt Hilda leaving the mansion to my side of the family?"

"Heavens yes. You have a passel of kids. I have no one to fill up this big hotel. And it would be heck to clean."

"You're sure –?"

"Don't give it another thought, sis. She left me Wabash Acres and other properties. Sound investments, that's more my style."

"Good," sighed Maddy just as Marybelle returned with a pot of hot tea. Oolong today.

After Marybelle placed the tray on a side table and poured two cups, Maddy turned to her sibling and asked, "Then, to what do I owe this visit?"

Maisie waited till the British woman was out of earshot, then blurted, "What does it mean for us that the Hoople Quadruplets were a fraud? Will we have to give our trust funds back? I've already donated a lot of mine to charities that are helping the town recover from the tornado. I could never afford to pay that money back."

"Calm down, my dear. I talked with Mark the Shark just last night. He assures me that all is still on the up and up. The trust funds, the mansion, the properties, the donations to charities – all that was Aunt Hilda's to do with as she chose."

"Even if she was a fake Hoople?"

"She wasn't a fake Hoople – she was adopted. She was a fake quadruple."

"So there's nothing for us to worry about?"

"Nothing ... other than the scandal."

"Scandal?"

"The Hoople family debunked the American public for over 80 years, profited from a false story. That won't play well on the six-o'clock news."

"Hm, I see your point. That might not be good for business at the café."

"Two points," said Maddy. "You weren't involved in the fraud. And you have enough money that you don't depend on the café for your well-being."

"But the shame –"

"There is that," Maddy admitted. "But the chicanery wasn't our doing, remember that."

"What about you and me? We're not even a legitimate family."

"Yes, dear, we are. You and I are the biological children of Howard Hoople and Sue Ann Polk."

"But Howard Hoople was merely Boy 1. He wasn't a real Hoople."

"Yes, he was. Like Aunt Hilda, he was legally adopted. He just wasn't the biological sibling of his adopted sisters. They were all legal Hooples – just not quadruplets."

"Oh. It's so confusing."

"The big question is how do we handle the news of the Hoople Quadruples being phony?" concluded Maddy with a dramatic wave of her hands. The motion sloshed the tea from her cup, leaving a spot on the carpet. No matter, Marybelle would take care of that. The dusty old Persian rug needed cleaning anyway. Maisie was right about this big house being difficult to keep clean. It would take an army of housekeepers to do it right. Thank goodness there was an upkeep fund that went with the mansion.

"Why does there have to be any news?" queried Maisie Walters. "Does anyone ever have to know?"

"I'm not sure. It may be an ethical question as much as a legal one."

The café owner leaned forward in her chair, carefully balancing her tea cup on her knee. "But why disappoint the American public? Why destroy the beautiful myth of the four quadruplets from a small Midwestern town? Why not allow Aunt Hilda to live out her life without being hassled by paparazzi or hounded by the news media over a fraud she had little control over? The quads were only children. Their parents did it."

Maddy considered this. "You make a good point. Aunt Hilda is the last of the Hoople Quadruples. After she's gone, it will only be a quaint story – like the Collyer Brothers or Lizzie Borden or P.T. Barnum's Fiji Mermaid."

"So we'll keep the story quiet?"

"Till after Aunt Hilda is gone. Then we'll revisit the subject."

"Who has to preserve the secret in the meantime?"

"Just the Quilters Club and our families. Plus Barnabas Soltairé and Aunt Hilda herself."

"And me."

"And you," nodded Maddy.

"Okay," agreed Maisie. "Let's give Aunt Hilda her remaining few years in peace. Then we'll tell the world."

~ ~ ~

Despite the drizzling rain, N'yen spent the day fishing with his Grampy and Uncle Edgar – Lizzie's husband. They huddled in the boat under umbrellas, pretty miserable as they trolled the muddy waters of the Wabash for catfish.

Predictably, N'yen caught the biggest fish; but according to tradition he released the bewhiskered bottom-feeder after measuring it at 18 inches. Not as large as Big Calvin, the elusive catfish under the Highway 101 Bridge, but not bad. Beau pulled in a 14 inch cat; Edgar got a 10 incher and a 12 incher. A good day in all.

Uncle Edgar's Jon boat sprang a leak but they plugged it using some of that waterproof tape you see on TV – the one where they cut out the bottom of a boat and replace it with a durable rubberized tape that instantly seals out water, air, and moisture to create a super strong, flexible, watertight barrier.

"We oughta star in one of those television commercials," said N'yen. Ignoring the fact that the Jon boat's leak was a tiny crack at a seam – cured by a band-aid-size strip of adhesive tape.

"Do a testimonial?" laughed Edgar Ridenour. "I look too much like a sasquatch to be seen on TV." His bushy beard and shaggy hair made his appearance quite fearsome.

"Wish I could find those secret papers," said the boy.

"What secret papers?" asked Edgar.

"There was a note with the Hoople birth certificates that suggested there might be more secret documents," explained Beau.

"What do you think these papers would be?" Edgar asked the boy. "Financial records? Deeds?"

"The note was in a box with the birth certificates. So I think it's something to do with the quadruplets. Maybe their adoption papers or more proof that they were just a big con game."

"It's hard to believe, four babies from separate families passed off as quadruplets. This could be quite a scandal."

"Only one left is Aunt Hilda. Maddy wants to wait until after she's gone before going public."

"Apparently, this fraud has been going on for 85 years. I suppose another year or two won't matter."

Chapter Twenty-Three

Tick Tock

"Did your sister Helga have any friends besides Floyd Hankins?" Maddy asked as they played checkers that rainy afternoon. Aunt Hilda was fond of board games. Outside the window the raindrops played a *tap-tap-tap* rhythm on the stone ledge.

"As I told you, we didn't have many friends. Mostly it was life on the road, one public appearance after another. We had a booking agent, you know. Tick Tock Dockery, we called him. Always consulting his watch, like he was late for an appointment. His real name was Thomas Dockery. He was on the family payroll. We had lots of help in the old days – booking agent, chaperon, chauffeur, cook, maid, valet, tutor, secretarial assistant."

"Now you have Marybelle," Maddy pointed out.

"Yes, she's practically all those things rolled into one!"

"Whatever happened to Tick Tock Dockery?" asked Maddy. Treading carefully with her questions while pretending to contemplate her next checker move. Addled mind or not, Aunt Hilda played a killer game.

"He's long dead, I'm sure. Otherwise, he'd be 105 by now."

"I suppose the same is true for all the old staff."

"Yes, all gone. None left except for Tick Tock's daughter. And Barney. He was the son of our housekeeper, such a cute little boy."

"Barnabas Soltairé, you mean?"

"Yes. But Barney was too young to play with. We were in our 20s when he was born. His father was a gypsy who sharpened knives door to door. I'm afraid that wayfaring miscreant took advantage of our poor Molly."

"Barnabas was illegitimate?"

"Yes. Some people say he's still a bastard," chuckled Aunt Hilda. "But he'll always be our little Barney Booger. That's what we called him."

"Barney Booger?"

"He was a cute little tyke. But at that age all we could do was bounce him on our knee."

"Tell me more about Tick Tock's daughter," Maddy said as she jumped one of Aunt Hilda's red checker buttons.

"A lovely girl. She used to come here with her dad. Played with us. We used to pretend she was one of us and call ourselves the Quintuplets. Those were merry days." She jumped two of Maddy's buttons in return. A good move.

Maddy cocked her head. "What was Mr. Dockery's daughter's name?"

"Marguerite, that was the little girl's name. When she grew up, she went off to Chicago to work for one of those alphabet companies."

"Alphabet companies?"

"You know, ABC or CBS or AT&T. Something like that. Got married, I heard, but then he died. She's a widow now."

"You've kept up with her?"

"No, no. But Helga did. Used to meet her for coffee."

"In Chicago?"

"No, here. Marguerite returned to Caruthers Corners

when she retired."

~ ~ ~

Aggie had just returned home from school. It was a short walk from Caruthers High, although the hike up Hoople Hill was a slog. She tossed her school books on a side table and wandered into the parlor to watch the checkers game.

"Grammy, I think Aunt Hilda has you on the run," the girl said as she studied the black-and-red board.

"Don't be so sure about that. I'm luring her into a trap," replied Maddy. Obviously bluffing.

"How's this for a trap?" laughed the old woman, clearing the board within the three next moves.

"How did you do that? I must be losing my touch."

"Ha! I was always the smartest of the Quadruples. None of my so-called sisters and brother could beat me at checkers."

"You said that you Hoople Quadruples knew you were frauds –" began Maddy.

Aunt Hilda stopped her. "We didn't think of ourselves as frauds. More like a vaudeville act. That was very common in show business, sister acts who weren't really related. Sister acts became quite popular during World War I, when there was a shortage of male performers. Women often teamed up as faux sister singing groups."

"Oh, I get it," said Aggie. "Like the Dixie Chicks? Only two of the trio are sisters."

"Yes, like that," nodded Aunt Hilda.

Aggie plowed on: "How about the Righteous Brothers. They weren't really brothers."

"But they *were* righteous," smiled Maddy. A longtime

fan of the singers who made "Unchained Melody" into a platinum hit.

"Or take the Three Stooges?" Aggie continued. "Larry Fine wasn't related to any of the other stooges – Moe Howard or Shemp Howard or later Curly Howard."

Maddy dredged up another example: "How about the Ramones. Joey Ramone was born Jeffrey Hyman, Johnny Ramone was born John Cummings."

"Is that true?" asked Aggie.

"I'm afraid so," said Maddy. She'd once seen the Ramones perform at New York's CBGB. "Matter of fact, none of the Ramones – Joey, Johnny, Dee Dee, Marky, C.J., Richie, Elvis, or Tommy –were actually related. They just shared the same stage name."

"Okay, okay," shushed Aunt Hilda. "You've proven my point. We Quadruples were merely performers on life's great stage."

Chapter Twenty-Four

Establishing Provenance

"I'm going to plan an exhibit around our Frank Leslie Quilt," announced Lizzie. "But we need to get it authenticated. I think I'll call in the Indianapolis Museum of Art to examine it."

"That's a good idea," agreed Cookie. "But first we'll need to establish its provenance."

"That may be difficult," replied Maddy, sipping her tea. The girls were sitting in the parlor at the Hoople Mansion and Marybelle had just prepared a fresh pot. "I found the quilt in the back of a closet here in this monster of a house. Aunt Hilda doesn't remember where it came from. It was probably collected by her mother, but there's no way to tell where *she* got it. Or who the quiltmaker was. So far, we've found no receipt for its purchase or letters that mention it or for that matter any hint of its existence."

"I haven't had any success either," said Cookie. "I've searched through the Historical Society files and all our old journals, but couldn't find any reference to a quilt like this."

"An appliqué using illustrations from *Leslie's Weekly* would be a big deal in the quilting world, especially one made nearly ten years before the Godey Quilt," declared Lizzie. "That would change quilting history."

"Yes," nodded Bootsie. "We have something significant here. This could put our little museum on the map."

"I know, I know," sighed Maddy. "But I'm not sure where to go from here."

Lizzie brushed the red strands of hair away from her face. As usual she wore makeup, her lips as crimson as a cherry tomato. "Are you sure Aunt Hilda can't remember anything more about the quilt?"

"Not really," replied Maddy. "The Parkinson's is taking its toll. The old girl gets confused a lot lately. She can barely tell which memories are true and which are imagined."

"That's a shame," said Bootsie. "I like Aunt Hilda."

"Me too," said Lizzie. "But we need to find out more about that quilt."

~ ~ ~

Marybelle Oliver got the assignment. She knew how to coax information out of Hilda Hoople. The elderly woman got confused under pressure. Having worked in the Hoople household for nearly a year now Marybelle had learned that it was best to approach queries from a side angle rather than straight on.

Instead of demanding "Do you remember seeing the quilt when you were a girl?" Marybelle took a different tact. Over a cuppa she casually said, "I'll bet your brother Howie was a handful."

"Yes," smiled the old woman as she blew on her tea to cool it, "Howie was always getting into trouble."

"Was your mother angry when he spilled chocolate on your sister Helga's quilt?"

"Oh, that wasn't Howie. That was that Tick Tock's daughter."

"Tick Tock?"

"Our booker – the man who set up our commercial

appearances. That's what we called him."

"His daughter sounds like she was a naughty little girl."

"Little girl? No, she was a teenager when she spilt that milkshake on Helga's quilt. Mother was very angry with her. Banned the girl from the Mansion."

~ ~ ~

Cookie did the math: If the booker's daughter was a teenager when she spilled that chocolate milkshake on what they were calling the Frank Leslie Quilt that would have made Helga around 19 or so. The Dockery girl had been a couple years younger than the quads. Now 85, Helga would have been 19 back in 1952. That was 27 years after the quilt was sewn, if you could trust the date stitched on the lower corner of the fabric.

If the booker's daughter was still alive, she might remember this incident that got her banned from the Hoople Mansion. She might even know where the quilt came from. It might be possible she'd remember the name of the quilter who made it.

But there was no one in Caruthers Corners named Marguerite Dockery.

Chapter Twenty-Five

The Unknown Quilter

The first hint as to the identity of the quiltmaker responsible for the Frank Leslie Quilt came from Aunt Hilda. "The bedroom where you found that decorated quilt used to be Helga's," she noted absently.

"Oh?"

"Yes, I had the room next to hers."

"I thought you said you saw the quilt in a guest bedroom."

"Did I? Maybe I was just confused. I'm pretty sure it was Helga's quilt."

"Was Helga the sister who died in the asylum?" asked Maddy. She had trouble keeping the quads straight.

"No, no. That was Helena. The poor girl was diagnosed as suffering from schizophrenia. A very sad case." She paused as if collecting her thoughts. "Helga is the sister who committed suicide by jumping in that geyser at Gruesome Gorge State Park back in '82."

"Why would Helga kill herself?"

"I think she was depressed over a failed romance."

"A romance with who?"

"She never said. But I suspected it was Floyd Hankins."

"You mean Sad Sammy Hankins' cousin? He died during the tornado."

"Yes, I heard. But 40 years ago he and Helga spent a lot

of time together on the church picnic committee. I think she had a big crush on him. I always wondered if perhaps she killed herself because Floyd wouldn't marry her."

"What makes you say that?"

"Just intuition. Helga and I were close."

"She was your favorite?"

"By default. Helena was moody and foul-tempered. Howie was busy carrying on with your mother. We had no other friends or playmates. Sometimes we saw the daughter of our booker. Or the maid's little boy, Barney."

"Yes, you told me about Barnabas Soltairé growing up here. The son of a gypsy knife-sharpener, you said."

"That's right. Or maybe he sold copper pans, I forget."

"It will come to you."

"Barney and his mother had the suite that N'yen is in. That wing was the servant's quarters back in the day."

"Tell me more about your booker's daughter," Maddy coaxed.

"Marguerite was closer to our age, maybe three or four years younger. She was fun to play with. But she was friendlier with Helga than anyone else."

"No other playmates?"

"Not really. We lived a very isolated life, home schooled, exhibited to strangers like zoo animals. No other acquaintances that I remember. But my memory's not what it used to be."

"Are you sure that quilt I found belonged to Helga?"

"You found it in her bedroom, so it was likely hers. But where she got it, I don't recall. I'd expect our mother gave it to her."

"Henrietta?"

"Yes, she's the one who doled out quilts and towels and bedsheets. Like War rations. You had to beg to get a fresh bath towel."

Perhaps it *was* War rationing, thought Maddy. The quads were preteens during World War II.

The old woman prattled on. "Our mother also picked out our clothing, making certain it all matched. We looked like we'd been stamped out of a die on a factory assembly line – all dressed alike, all duplicates of each other."

"She may have dressed you children alike, but you had nothing else in common. All of you were adopted from different mothers."

"Stolen, is more like it. I always wondered who my mother really was."

"There's no way to tell from the birth certificates. They list the mothers' names, but it's anybody's guess whether you were Girl 1 or Girl 2 or Girl 3."

"That's true, but you should be able to trace *your* bloodline."

"Me? How so?"

"Because there was only one Boy 1 certificate. That had to be Howie. And, as you say, the certificate lists the name of the birth mother."

That stopped Maddy. She hadn't thought of that. The answer was so simple. "You're right," she said. "I can determine *my* lineage."

"That is, if you're still want to know. At my age, I don't think it would make any difference. Everybody but me is likely to be long gone."

"I admit I'm curious. I'll look at that certificate again. I didn't pay attention when we first examined them."

"Where are the birth certificates?"

"We put the box back in the safe. That seemed as good a place to store the papers as any."

"Just don't shut the door. You'll never be able to open it again."

"You're sure you don't have the combination written down anywhere?"

"Possibly, but I don't remember. Things have been fuzzy lately."

"Have you been taking your Levodopa?" Levodopa, also known as L-DOPA, is considered one of the most effective drugs for treating Parkinson's Disease. The brain cells change it into dopamine, a neuro-transmitter necessary for controlling balance and motor coordination.

"It gives me nausea. No wonder they call it Dope."

"That's a common symptom," Maddy conceded. "But it's better than having tremors and stiff muscles." No need to mention hallucinations and delusions. Aunt Hilda was already starting to show signs.

"Nobody else in the family ever had Parkinson's," she grumbled.

"Parkinson's in not an inherited disease. Besides, none of you were actually brother and sister – remember?" Conversations with Aunt Hilda were becoming more difficult.

The old woman sighed and took a sip of her Chamomile tea. "There's one good thing about my brother and sisters not being related."

"What's that?"

"Helena was diagnosed with schizophrenia. Some people say that disease is genetic. But since Helena and I weren't actually related, I didn't have to worry about inheriting that sad affliction."

"True."

"Also, Helga suffered from depression, but not me. I was always a happy-go-lucky sort. And your father, he was a jerk. Thank goodness, there's no catching that!"

"See, you have no traits in common with your fake siblings."

"I'm certainly glad about that. I never cared for any of them. Disagreeable people, one and all. Funny, how everybody always said we looked so much alike."

"The power of suggestion, I suppose. Your mother always dressed you alike."

"Perhaps. But I always thought I was the prettiest sister."

~ ~ ~

For her age, Maddy Madison was an attractive woman. Her silver-gray hair framed an oval face. She'd added a few pounds, but her figure was pleasantly curvy.

On the other hand, her daughter Tilly was quite slender, taking after her beanpole father. Even four children hadn't distorted her youthful shape. A pretty blonde, she had the grace and carriage of a fashion model.

Aggie looked like she might take after her grandmother. Her prepubescent body was starting to fill out. She was now wearing a training bra – although she wasn't sure why her new boobies needed to be "trained."

Maddy was disappointed that she didn't favor her Aunt Hilda, a trim, spry little woman, despite her 85 years. But if the quads weren't biological siblings, that would explain the difference in appearance.

Oh well, Pooh Bear – Beau, that is – assured her that he liked her just the way she was! Nonetheless, she wouldn't mind losing a few pounds. That was hard to do. She so loved watermelon cake.

Chapter Twenty-Six

Business in a Small Town

Justin Harribald didn't get released from jail as planned. When that sleazy lawyer from Burpyville tried to serve the Writ, Chief Purdue phoned Mark Tidemore for help. He'd already been burned once by J. Harold Wentworth's shenanigans. Not again, he told himself.

Mark was happy to assist his police chief. He'd phoned Hamilton Greenwald over in Burpyville for a mayor-to-mayor talk. And Greenwald had phoned Judge John Lawrence Bristol for a little heart-to-heart. And the Writ was withdrawn.

It was simply a matter of pressure. Mark the Shark had threatened to leak the word that Ham Greenwald had a mistress, a local Amway sales lady named Francine Jenkins. This wasn't the sort of news Ham's wife would welcome. In turn, Ham Greenwald threatened to kick Judge Bristol out of the weekly poker game if he didn't back off on this *habeas corpus* business.

As a result, the judge withdrew the Writ but kept the $15 grand.

J. Harold Wentworth kept the $10-.

Ralph Aitken found himself out $25-.

And Justin Harribald remained in jail.

That's the way business gets done in a small town.

~ ~ ~

Facing a possible manslaughter charge, Harribald began talking. An easy give, he turned in the kid who acted as courier between the meth lab and the Indy boys.

Chief Purdue immediately recognized the name, a local juvie named Theodore DiMacchio. He'd questioned Teddy D only a few days ago, but there wasn't anything to hold him on. It isn't illegal for your car to be spotted three blocks from a crime scene. But now the pieces were starting to fit together.

Teddy D was a drug runner. A shame, for the DiMacchios were good people. His father owned a tire store out near the Industrial Park that had been wiped out by the recent tornado. Now this.

Chief Purdue immediately called Judge Harry Cramer and got a warrant to pick the boy up. Although Indiana's forfeiture law says cars can be seized without a warrant if they are used "to transport or in any manner facilitate the transportation" of drugs, a US District Chief Judge had ruled last year that Indiana's forfeiture law violates the due process clause of the Fifth and Fourteenth Amendments of the US Constitution. A warning sign for the state's lawmen.

That's why Chief Purdue was careful to follow the rules. The Fourth Amendment of the U.S. Constitution ensures the right of every American "to be secure in their persons, houses, papers, and effects, against unreasonable searches and seizures," with the added assurance that "no warrants shall issue" without probable cause. That is reiterated under Article I, Section 11 of the Indiana Constitution.

Judge Cramer agreed the sworn statement of Justin Harribald was strong enough to show probable cause. He was known to be a police-friendly jurist.

Warrant in hand, Deputy Truehart took Teddy D into custody. He also impounded Teddy's new Infiniti QX60.

Herman Vox was called in to examine the car. The CSI tech found traces of N-methamphetamine in the trunk's felt lining. Thus, Teddy D was formally arrested and his car became property of the state.

The War On Drugs Asset Forfeiture laws allow the police to hold onto property if the owner is engaged in illegal activities like using a car to transport meth. The vehicle is usually put up for auction to the highest bidder.

In most states, the money from an auction goes to buy bullet-proof vests and other police equipment. However, in Indiana no forfeiture proceeds are allowed to go to law enforcement. Too bad. The Caruthers Corners Police Department operated on a belt-tight budget.

At any rate, Teddy DiMacchio wouldn't have a need for his fancy automobile. He'd be locked away in prison, unable to cruise the streets of Caruthers Corners and Pitsville like a pimp on parade.

~ ~ ~

Despite Teddy D being a local boy from a good family, Chief Purdue leaned on him hard. Drugs – whether the manufacturing, transportation, or distribution – had no place in his town.

Crystal meth is a version of the drug methamphetamine. It can be taken by snorting, smoking or injecting it. The drug creates a high – an euphoric rush with an intense sense of happiness, well-being, and confidence. The effects last around six to eight hours.

Being a stimulant, meth is often used as a party drug because of the energy it creates, allowing people to dance for long periods of time.

Crystal meth is considered incredibly dangerous and addictive. Not only can the drug produce aggressive and psychotic behaviors, it can also damage a user's heart and brain.

Although it has effects similar to cocaine, meth is a synthetic drug made from chemicals. A process called "cooking" is often used to produce meth. It begins with extracting ephedrine or pseudoephedrine from cold or diet medicines. A chemical reaction is created by adding such ingredients as ammonia and lithium. A solvent is then added to extract the meth. Acidic gas going through the meth creates the crystals.

As part of the Combat Methamphetamine Act of 2005, Congress set requirements that retailers and pharmacies must track the purchase of products like pseudoephedrine that are used to make the drug. It also places limits on the amount of certain over-the-counter medicines people can purchase in one day.

Meth makers get around it by using "smurfs," multiple people paid to buy up to the legal limit and turn the cold medicine over to the illegal lab.

The process of making meth is dangerous, mainly because the materials are flammable and explosive.

Some of the dangerous ingredients include:

- Acetone, which is found in nail polish remover and paint thinner;
- Anhydrous ammonia, which is found in window cleaners and fertilizer;
- Hydrochloric acid, a substance that's corrosive and can eat away flesh;

- Lithium, which is explosive and can cause burns to the skin;
- Red phosphorous, which is very flammable;
- Sulfuric acid, which is commonly used in drain cleaners and can burn skin.

Signs of a meth lab can be an odor like paint or a "hospital smell." In some cases, meth smells like vinegar or ammonia.

However, when meth is smoked, it tends to have an almost sweet smell.

Chief Purdue thought locking up drug dealers was pretty sweet too.

Chapter Twenty-Seven

Red Flags

Teddy D spilled his guts, naming three other meth manufacturers in Caruthers County. Except for one, these were Small Production Capacity Labs (SPCLs) – "One Pot" and "Shake & Bake" labs with one-gram to multigram yields. All had been backed by the late Boyd Aikens.

One of these labs had been operated by Floyd Hankins, Sad Sammy's cousin. But Floyd had died in the twister that hit them back in September. So that facility was already closed down.

Another was the work of Buddy Flynn's youngest brother, a loser known as Little Joe. A small guy, he'd been nicknamed after that cowboy on *Bonanza*. It had been popular on TV when he was a teenager. Now in his 30s, he'd had no known means of support – until now. Judging by the decaying teeth of his "meth mouth," he used more of the product than he sold. Deputy Petie Hitzer picked him up. They had gone to high school together. They had been on the track team together. But Little Joe didn't try to run. He held out his hands for the cuffs, saying, "You got me fair and square, bro."

The third lab belonged to an old hermit known locally as Possum. He lived in a shack on the far side of Never Ending Swap. His was by far the biggest operation. A typical SPCL meth lab might turn out about 5,000 grams per batch.

But working day and night, Possum's 22-liter setup averaged close to 50,000 grams. Petie picked up Possum and his two helpers too.

This was a big score for a small-town police department.

Nonetheless, Chief Purdue called in the Feds. The FBI had more jails cells at its disposal than the Caruthers Corner Police Department. Jim's two holding cells were already occupied, with Justin Harribald in one, Jasper Beanie sleeping off a drunk in the other.

The FBI loved getting into a case ahead of the DEA. Special Agent in Charge Neil Wannamaker now owed Jim a big favor.

~ ~ ~

Police look for certain red flags that tip them off to possible meth labs. In addition to ammonia or "paint" smells, signs of a meth lab can include odd activities late at night, people who seem to be unemployed but have plenty of money, or people who act overly paranoid. The curtains of a house with a meth lab are often drawn. And residents go outside to smoke a cigarette rather than doing it inside. There might be dead spots in the lawn where chemical waste has been dumped. Or there could be a lot of bottles and plastic containers piled in the trash.

Jim Purdue chastised himself for not picking up on the four meth labs in his jurisdiction. Possum's was understandable, his shack near the Swamp being remote and unvisited. But there was no excuse for missing Mr. Harribald's or the other two. Floyd's was right there on his farm. And Little Joe's was in the barn on the old Flynn homeplace.

He missed the old days when his biggest drug bust was a few marijuana plants growing in the backyard of Herbie Benson, a local stoner and subscriber to *High Times* magazine.

Fritz Berber, the mailman, had tipped the police off to Herbie's magazine subscription. Herbie was harmless, growing weed for his own consumption. Jim always cut down the offending stalks, but left him enough seed to replant.

~ ~ ~

N'yen spent a lot of time on his souped-up Dell Precision 7730 computer. His Grammy had arranged for AT&T to install a high-speed 100 Mbps Internet hookup for him. A bribe to prolong his visits. She had loved it when the boy lived with her and Beau full-time during that period Bill and Kathy had been on the outs.

When N'yen wasn't hacking into corporate databases or government agencies, he liked to spend his time fishing on the Wabash with his Grampy and Uncle Edgar. He could usually out-fish them, thanks to a little coaching from his Uncle Jim. People often forgot that before Jim Purdue took up law enforcement, he'd spent his early years as a professional fishing guide. That was when Beau and Edgar had been in Vietnam; but he'd had flat feet.

And now James Lester Purdue was a flat foot, to use the local parlance.

The boy admired his Uncle Jim's career choice. That's why he liked solving crimes with the Quilters Club. It was almost like being a lawman himself.

N'yen was good at outthinking crooks. His Grammy was pretty good at it too, but sometimes she could use a little help. Aggie wasn't bad at catching crooks either, but she was getting distracted lately by that ooky Bobby Elwood. What did she see in that jerk anyway?

N'yen had been giving a lot of thought to the message he'd found in the bottom of the rosewood box that held the birth certificates. SECRET PAPERS IN VAULT, it read. They had looked top-to-bottom throughout the Herring-Hall-Marvin double-door safe without finding any other papers that looked "secret." Maybe somebody had already removed them. The safe doors had been standing open when Aggie found it.

Nonetheless N'yen was determined to figure this out before going back to Chicago. Aggie would never do it on her own, off playing kissy-face with Bobby Elwood.

Yuck!

Chapter Twenty-Eight

Calling Up Old Ghosts

Everybody gathered around the big dining room table as if participating in a séance – Maddy and Beau, Tilly and Mark, Freddie and Amanda, even Maisie Walters. The Quilters Club members and their spouses were there too.

Aunt Hilda had already gone to bed, so Marybelle volunteered to watch the little children.

That didn't include Aggie and N'yen, both of whom had demanded a front row seat. "After all, I'm the one who found the birth certificates," Aggie declared as she scooted her chair closer to the long oak table. "And I want to know who my great-great grandmother was."

This was the "official" unveiling of Maddy's true family tree.

She had grown up thinking she was a Taylor. Her grandmother had been Madelyn Taylor – or so she'd been told.

Then for the last few years she had come to believe she was a Hoople. But now it appeared that Henrietta Hoople wasn't really her grandmother.

Third time's the charm, she told herself as she carefully opened the rosewood box that held the birth certificates of the four "quadruplets."

"Hurry it up, mom," whispered Tilly. "The suspense is driving me nuts. Are we descended from Town Founders or

White Trash?"

"Here goes," said Maddy, thumbing through the papers until she came to the one labeled Boy 1. Holding it up to the light, she read the name aloud: "Sarah Celine Jinks."

This was a showstopper.

"T-that can't be right," stuttered Maddy, looking down to examine the name again. But there it was: Sarah Celine Jinks, age 14.

That was Granny Crackleton's maiden name ... before she married Happy Howard Crackleton and started that lineage of inbred looneys.

No, this couldn't be right.

Beau stepped forward to steady his wife. Tilly looked horror-stricken. Maisie ran toward the bathroom, making retching sounds. Aggie looked puzzled. Being adopted, N'yen knew the bloodline didn't apply to him.

"Mom, are you all right?" asked Freddie.

"We're Crackletons," she gasped. As if declaring the End of the World.

Lizzie blurted, "All the Crackletons are crazy as bedbugs."

"Maddy's not crazy," protested Bootsie. "She's the sanest person I know – maybe."

This is not good news," concluded Cookie. She was already rearranging family trees in her head.

Maddy took a deep breath, realizing she had just discovered Barnabas Soltairé's Secret Number Two. She was a "Cuckoo for Cocoa Puffs" Crackleton.

~ ~ ~

Cookie took charge. "Here," she demanded, "let me see that birth certificate." As local historian, she knew practically every genealogy chart in the entire county. There had to be some mistake here. Granny Crackleton had only three children – Jebediah, Claude, and Faith Ann.

Maddy handed over the yellowed paper. Her hand was shaking. She looked as if about to cry.

"Hmm," muttered Cookie, as she examined the document. "There are more than 6,000 entities in the US that issue birth certificates. But I don't see a stamp indicating any of these certificates were ever filed with the United States Public Health Service."

"Does that mean it's fake?" asked Maddy, hopefully.

Mark looked over Cookie's shoulder. "No," he said. "That's only been a requirement since 1946. These certificates predated that rule."

"Not being registered might be to your favor if you really want to know your lineage," observed N'yen.

"What do you mean?" asked Maddy.

"When an adoption is finalized, the government usually seals the original birth certificate and issues a replacement certificate substituting the individual's birth name with the name selected by the adoptive parents. It also replaces the birth parent's name with that of the adoptive parents. In many cases, adoptees are not granted access to their own original birth certificate."

"You're saying that if these birth certificates had gone through official channels we still wouldn't have the names of the mothers."

"Not likely."

"How do you know this?"

"Because I'm adopted," he reminded them. As if his yellow-cast skin and epicanthic eyelids weren't giveaway enough in this Anglo-Saxon gathering.

"Maybe it would've been better not to know," said Maddy.

"C'mon, it's not so bad. The Jinks are descended from a Town Founder," said Cookie, trying to put a positive spin on this news.

"Yes, but Granny married into the Crackletons," Lizzie pointed out. "Tainted seed."

"Thanks for the clarification," muttered Maddy, not meaning it.

"But if Granny was only 14 when Howie was born, that might mean his father wasn't a Crackleton," said Cookie. "She didn't marry Happy Howard until she was 18 or 19; the records aren't clear."

"Then why name the baby after Happy Howard?" countered Bootsie.

"Does the birth certificate name a father?" asked Mark.

Maddy shook her head, silver hair glinting in the light of the overhead chandelier. "No, all four certificates say FATHER UNKNOWN."

"Should we check the records at the Town Hall?" suggested Freddie. "There might be more information there."

"Doubt that will help," said Mark. "Like Cookie said, a certified birth certificate has a registrar's embossed seal, registrar's signature, and the date that the certificate was filed with the registrar's office. This one has none of that. So I'd guess Rev. David Dimpledorf's Caring Home For Unwed Mothers never bothered to file it."

"Not registered?" said Maddy. "Does that mean my lineage doesn't officially exist?"

"Oh, we know Granny Crackleton exists," said Aggie brightly. "She's probably sitting on her front porch in Crackleton Crossing at this very minute."

"Yeah," said N'yen. "She's probably sitting there muttering, '*Double, double, toil and trouble.*'"

~ ~ ~

Later that night Beau found his wife sitting dejectedly in the Mansion's library. A big cavernous room, it was lined with books on three sides. She hadn't bothered to turn the lights on. Her silhouette could have passed for an abandoned statue. Or a forlorn ghost. Her husband quietly called out, "Why so glum, dear?"

"Because I've discovered that I'm a Crackleton. That's enough to depress anyone."

"Relax. You're who you are. And the same person you've always been."

"Pooh Bear, I'm not sure what you just said, but I'll take it as a compliment."

"I thought it sounded better than saying 'There, there.'"

"I can't believe that Granny Crackleton is my grandmother. That would mean I helped send my uncle to jail."

"Jeb, you mean."

"Yes, Jebediah Crackleton *and* his three sons – my cousins, it would seem."

"How about Faith Ann? That would make her son your cousin." Gus Crackleton was the kid being fostered by Cookie and her husband Ben.

"Oh my," moaned Maddy. "This is getting a bit too close to home."

"I'm just glad you didn't get any of the Crackletons' crazy

genes."

"Are you sure about that?"

"After forty years of marriage, I think I would've noticed by now."

"You mean I'm not 'Cuckoo for Cocoa Puffs'?" That was the derisive chant school kids used for the Crackletons.

"At least none of our children are dwarfs or giants or have two heads."

"Sometimes I'm not so sure about Bill." That was N'yen's adoptive dad. Bill was the son with the airy do-gooder brain. More good intentions than smarts.

"Are you going to talk with her?"

"Talk with who?"

"Your biological grandmother. Your father's real mother – Sarah Celine Crackleton."

"Why should I? I've already met the old witch."

"Are there no questions you want to ask her – like why she gave your dad up for adoption?"

"The answer's pretty evident. According to the birth certificate, she was only 14 at the time."

Beau looked up. "Younger than Aggie," he said.

"Don't say that. I'm worried enough about Mark and Tilly letting her date. She's just a child."

"Aggie's got a sound head on her shoulders. And Bobby Elwood's a good kid. I know his dad."

"Hormones are hormones," she shook her head knowingly.

"I vaguely recall," he chuckled.

"I'll think about it," she said.

"About what? Aggie's dating?"

"No, talking with Granny Crackleton."

Chapter Twenty-Nine

Leslie's Weekly

The Quilters Club met for breakfast at Cozy Café. Aggie was in school. N'yen was off fishing with his Grampy and Uncle Edgar – his parents were still at that conference in Colorado. The gals had gathered to talk about the Frank Leslie Quilt. They were no closer to establishing its provenance than when Maddy had found it there in the back of a closet in the Hoople Mansion.

"The quilt has the date 1925 sewn into a corner," Lizzie pointed out. "That's highly unusual. Seamstresses don't usually date their quilts. We never do."

"Actually, the Godey's Quilt has a date on it. The final version included the text, 'Mildred Potter Lissauer/Her Quilt/1934,' "

"Huh," said Lizzie. "That's news to me." She prided her knowledge in quilting lore. But it was hard to outdo her friend's unfailing memory.

Cookie said, "What puzzles me more are those fashion silhouettes from *Leslie's Weekly*."

"What's puzzling about that?" replied Lizzie. "The magazine didn't cease publication until 1922. There would've been plenty of copies still around. People didn't start getting rid of their magazines until the paper drives of World War II."

"That's not the problem."

"Then – prey tell – what is?" You could see the redhead was getting exasperated with Cookie's comments.

"Most of the illustrations are women's portraits based on magazine covers from the 1920s – or before – but one is clearly recognizable as Amelia Earhart."

"So –?" said Lizzie.

"Earhart didn't become internationally famous until 1928, when she became the first woman passenger to make a Transatlantic flight with Wilmer Stultz. That was three years after the date on the quilt."

"Was it a *Leslie's Weekly* cover?"

"No, a *McCall's* cover. May 1937."

Lizzie looked pained. "But that's 12 years after the date stitched on the quilt."

"My point exactly."

"W-what?" gulped Bootsie.

Lizzie was speechless.

As usual, Maddy kept her wits about her. "That means the quilt has to be a fake," she said.

"Fake, fake, bake me a cake," Cookie chanted an old jump-rope rhyme. "We've been bamboozled."

~ ~ ~

"Okay, are you saying someone put a fake quilt in that closet for Maddy to find?" asked Bootsie. The cop's wife sniffing for a misdeed.

"No," replied Cookie. "I'm just saying this quilt didn't predate the Godey's Quilt."

"But what about the date stitched in the corner."

"That's the puzzler."

"Let's examine the quit more closely," said Lizzie,

placing an 8" x 10" photo in the center of the Formica table, careful not to spill any coffee on it. This was one of the pix she'd hired Bob "Flash" Dougan to take. She'd been planning to send it down to the Indianapolis Museum of Art to start the authentication process. But that plan looked pretty dead at the moment.

Amelia Earhart indeed!

Lizzie carefully scrutinized each of the fifteen images appliquéd onto the peach-colored fabric. "Not my personal taste in quilt design, but it *is* a pretty good knock-off of the Godey Quilt."

"Fooled me too," said Bootsie, wrinkling her pug nose.

"But it offers a nice selection of images," observed Cookie.

Lizzie said to her friend, "How so?"

"All of them are covers from *Leslie's Weekly* – or its sister publications – except for the one *McCall's*."

"Can you tell us which issues they're based on?"

"No problem," said the blonde. She studied the photo for a few minutes, then began her recitation: "The woman with a headband was the cover of the October 2, 1920, issue of *Leslie's Weekly*. As you can see, it's promoting women to vote in the first Presidential election since the Nineteenth Amendment."

"That's the Amendment to the US Constitution that gave us gals the vote, right?" said Bootsie.

"Actually, it prohibits the states and the federal government from denying the right to vote to citizens of the United States on the basis of sex," clarified Maddy. Sort of a backward way of saying the same thing.

Cookie continued, "This next appliqué has the same

theme, a woman holding a ballot. It comes from the August 7, 1920, cover of *Leslie's Illustrated Weekly Newspaper.*"

"Keep going," encouraged Lizzie, leaning closer to look at the tiny images.

Cookie traced her finger across the photo. "This one, a woman posing as Columbia, that's also from 1920." She paused to get her breath. "And this woman sitting on a teetertotter is from the May 15, 1920 issue of *Leslie's Weekly.*"

"A lot of these illustrations are from the early '20s," noted Bootsie.

"The problem is this one." Cookie pointed at the image in the lower right of the quilt. "This is obviously Amelia Earhart. But nobody knew who she was in the early '20s."

Maddy summed it up. "You're saying if this quilt was made in 1925 this portrait of Amelia Earhart is an impossibility. It's from an issue of *McCall's* published 12 years after the date on the quilt."

Everybody studied the glossy photograph sadly. All hopes of a great discovery dashed by one anachronistic image out of the 15 appliqués.

~ ~ ~

Lizzie asked, "Are you sure this Amelia Earhart appliqué comes from a 1937 issue of McCall's? Maybe you're remembering the cover or date wrong?"

"No, I've got it right. The cover portrait was painted by Neysa McMein. She was a successful magazine illustrator who also painted portraits of presidents, actors, and writers. Born as Marjorie Frances McMein in 1888, she changed her name to Neysa on the advice of a numerologist. A beautiful redhead, she was a regular member of the famous Algonquin Round Table."

"Okay. Your point?"

"From 1923 through 1937, Neysa McMein created all of *McCall's* covers – including the May 1937 Amelia Earhart cover."

"That was the same portrait of Amelia Earhart depicted on the quilt here?"

"Yes," Cookie nodded. "Under her portrait was the cover line: 'America's great women: Amelia Earhart, who spanned an ocean and won a world.' At the time *McCall's* was being promoted as 'Three Magazines in One.' Each of the three sections – News and Fiction, Homemaking, Style and Beauty –had its own cover and contained ads tailored to the specific contents. That was the year the magazine started printing a complete novel in each issue. The cover price was ten cents. There's a tiny image of a twin-engine airplane on the lower left corner of the cover – a Lockheed Electra, I believe." She paused. "Does that convince you?"

Maddy shook her head with admiration. "How do you do that?"

"Do what?" responded Cookie. Perhaps a little disingenuously.

"Remember all these stray facts."

"I've been able to do this all my life. You know that."

"It still mystifies me. You're like Miss Memory."

Cookie smiled impishly. "Do you mean Mr. Memory from Alfred Hitchcock's *The 39 Steps*? Released in 1935, starring Robert Donat and Madeleine Carroll. The British Film Institute ranked it as fourth best British film of the 20th Century."

"Show off," said Bootsie.

"If you're so smart," said Maddy, "who played Mr. Memory?"

"That's easy – Wylie Watson."

"I don't know if you're right or not," Maddy admitted.

"Trust me, I'm right," winked Cookie.

Maisie walked over to refill their coffee cups from a fresh pot. Cozy Café had a reputation for keeping the Maxwell House flowing – only 50-cent for a "never-ending cup." That and watermelon pie were its main attractions.

"You oughta be a contestant on *Jeopardy*," said Maisie. "That's quite a knack."

Cookie blushed. "I can't explain it. Facts stick to my mind like flypaper."

"I can explain it," teased Maddy. "It's a genetic mutation. She's like the X-Men." Aggie and N'yen were big fans of movies based on Marvel Comics.

"Mutation?" laughed Maisie. "Hate to say this, Cookie Bentley, but it sounds like you're a better candidate for being descended from the Crackletons than me and Maddy."

"Hey, don't try to connect me with that pack of loonies," rejoined the blonde. Then catching herself, she tried to backpedal. "Uh, no insult intended."

"Like fudge," said Maddy. But she wasn't angry. She had accepted the twisted branches of her family tree.

~ ~ ~

According to the doctors that Katherine "Cookie" Bentley consulted (neuroscientists, actually), there were several different types of super memory:

Hyperthymia – This is sometimes called Autobiographical Memory. It's a condition that enables certain people to remember almost all their life experiences in vivid detail. What happened on a specific date, the room number from a one-time hotel stay, what you ate for breakfast on a given day in the past. It's like being a "human diary." A very rare condition.

Hypermnesia exhibits occasional instances of enhanced memory, "a few spot islands of pristine recall in an ocean of otherwise ordinarily incomplete memories." Everyone experiences this from time to time – a beach trip, a particular high school class, a long-ago play date with friends, events that stick out in your memory with clarity. Hypermnesia is a fairly common experience.

Flashbulb Memories – This is the ability to recall very emotionally charged events in your life (like what you were doing when 9/11 happened or where you were when JFK was assassinated). It's common for most everybody.

Savant Syndrome is a disorder often linked with autism or Asperger's. A good example is Kim Peek, the savant on whom the *Rain Man* movie was based. An atypical memory is often associated with this neurodevelopmental disorder.

Mnemonics refers to special techniques used to enhance one's recall. "Memory tricks," some people call it. Word and image association can help improve prospective memory, procedural memory, semantic memory, or autobiographical memory. This is the result of training one's memory, rather than being born with a special talent.

A Thimbleful of Murder

According to the docs, Cookie had what's known as an **Eidetic Memory** – more commonly called a **Photographic Memory**. This is the ability to accurately recall images, sounds, pages of text, or numbers for long periods of time – days, weeks, years. These memory feats are similar to a savant's, but without the autistic symptoms.

Ever since childhood, Cookie had exhibited Total Recall, the ability to pull up a memory in perfect detail. She had no idea why she could do this. There had been no precipitating traumatic event, no injury, no known causation.

However, this wasn't a bad talent for a historian to have, the enhanced capability to recall names and dates and stray facts. She was a whiz at *Trivial Pursuit*.

Cookie knew she wasn't some kind of genius. Her brain worked about the same as any other middle-aged woman – it was just that she could remember things.

Chapter Thirty

Helga's Coffee Pal

"Let's get back to the quilt," insisted Lizzie. "Where did this illustration come from?" She pointed to the second appliqué in row two of the photograph.

Cookie followed her friend's well-manicured fingernail. "Oh, the Red Cross nurse comes from the September 18, 1917, edition of *Leslie's Weekly.*"

"And the female Santa?"

"That one's from December 1, 1917."

"*Leslie's Weekly* – what's the publication's history?" asked Maisie Walters, intrigued by this recitation of facts.

"*Leslie's Weekly* actually began in 1855 as *Frank Leslie's Illustrated Newspaper,*" responded Cookie. "He also published such titles as *Frank Leslie's Ladies' Gazette of Fashion and Fancy Needlework, Frank Leslie's Popular Monthly, Frank Leslie's Ladies' Journal, Frank Leslie's Lady's Magazine, Frank Leslie's New Family Magazine, Frank Leslie's Fact and Fiction, Frank Leslie's Home Library, Frank Leslie's New York Journal of Romance, Frank Leslie's Boys' and Girls' Weekly, Frank Leslie's Children's Friend, Frank Leslie's Chimney Corner, Frank Leslie's Pleasant Hours (for Boys and Girls).*"

"Whew! One thing you can say about Frank Leslie," observed Bootsie, "he certainly liked the sound of his own name."

"Not only him," laughed Cookie. "When he died in 1880, his second wife legally changed her name to 'Frank Leslie' and continued publishing the magazine."

~ ~ ~

"Hey Maisie," said her sister. "Did Helga Hoople ever come in here for coffee?"

"Sure. Although I didn't know she was my aunt back then."

"What brings up Helga Hoople?" asked Lizzie. "She committed suicide more than three decades ago."

"That's right," nodded Bootsie. "She jumped in the geyser at the State Park. It was one of Jim's first cases. The body was never recovered. The family had to hold an empty casket funeral."

"Something Aunt Hilda said about her sister," replied Maddy. "It has to do with the Frank Leslie Quilt." Turning back to Maisie, she continued, "Do you remember if anyone ever met Aunt Helga for coffee?"

Maisie scrunched up her face to think. "You're talking nearly forty years ago. I'd just started waitressing here – straight out of high school. That's lotsa cups of coffee ago."

"Picture it in your head," coaxed Maddy. "Did she sit by herself or did someone join her?"

"Now that I think about it, she sometimes met Rita Rutaberger. Rita came back to town after she retired from IBM."

Bingo! thought Maddy. IBM – an alphabet company. "Did she used to be Marguerite Dockery?"

"That's right. Thomas Dockery's daughter. She married a Chicago man named Rutaberger, but he died on her."

"So Marguerite is called Rita now?"

Maisie nodded. "Yes, she came back from Chicago using the shortened version of her name."

"I guess they're more casual in the big city," surmised Cookie. Ignoring the fact that she was no longer Katherine or that Bootsie had given up Barbara or Lizzie didn't go by Elizabeth. Even Maddy and Maisie weren't called Madelyn and Margaret these days.

"I've never been to Chicago," said Maisie.

"You should go sometime," Maddy advised her twin. "It's only 200 miles from here."

"Who's got the time, running the diner and all?"

Cookie said, "You'd enjoy the view from Willis Tower. At 1,730 feet, it's the second tallest building in the US."

"Didn't that used to be the Sears Tower?"

"Right. They changed the name in 2009."

"Rita Rutaberger," said Bootsie. "Didn't she fall and break her hip during the tornado?"

"Yes," confirmed Lizzie. She kept up on all the local gossip. "There were complications, bad bones or something. I think they still have her in Burpyville Memorial."

"Hmm," Maddy gave it some thought. You could almost hear the gears turning. "You know what," she said, "I think we ought to pay Helga's friend Rita a hospital visit."

"Do we need to bring flowers?" asked Bootsie.

Chapter Thirty-One

Broken Hip

Rita Rutaberger (née Dockery) lay in a hospital bed under whiter-than-snow sheets, reading the latest issue of *Journal of Computer and System Sciences*. Exciting reading for nerds and techies, no doubt. As well as retired IBM professionals.

They had found her in the rehab wing of Burpyville Memorial.

Each year about 300,000 Americans – most of them over age 65 – break a hip. It happens to women more often than men. That's because women fall more often and are more likely to have osteoporosis, a disease that makes bones weak.

Rita's recovery had been slow. She was still using a walker.

"Didn't drink enough milk as a child," she offered a self-diagnosis to her visitors. "Got a bad case of osteoporosis as a result. Pins have trouble holding in crumbly old bones."

The woman was as thin as a broomstick, with short white hair sticking up on her scalp like a wire brush. She wore a yellow nightgown that hung loosely on her skeletal frame. Her pale skin looked as if it had never been exposed to sunlight.

"We brought you these flowers," said Maddy, handing her a bouquet of daffodils. The tornado had wiped out the only flower shop in Caruthers Corners, so they had picked up these yellow blossoms at a kiosk in the hospital's lobby.

"Thank you kindly, ladies. These are the first flowers I've received since I've been in this disinfectant-reeking prison. I don't have too many friends left, being 82 and having spent my working career with IBM in Chicago. Not many people remember me."

"We heard you used to be friends with the Hoople Quadruples," said Bootsie in her brash manner. "That's what we came to ask you about."

"That – and to check on your recovery," Maddy hastily amended. Softening the request.

"The Hoople kids? Yes, I knew them. My father booked their appearances. Sometimes he let me accompany him to the Mansion. A big ol' place. The quads were two or three years older than me, but we got on pretty well. After I came back from Chicago, me and Helga continued to get together until – well, until what happened to her."

"Yes, it was a tragedy, dying that way," nodded Cookie. "I understand the body was never recovered."

"Well, of course not. That Blow Hole is bottomless."

Cookie was about to correct her, but thought better of it. The US Corps of Engineers had measured the Blow Hole a few years back, confirming its depth at 675 feet. A crack in the tectonic plate that allowed the heated waters from deep inside the earth to come roiling up in the form of a puny, gurgling geyser.

Tucked away in the far corner of a canyon in Gruesome Gorge State Park, the hot springs has been closed off to the public since Helga Hoople's untimely demise. A chain blocks the pathway and a rusted sign warns the public away. A safety precaution by the Indiana Department of Natural Resources.

"There's something I wanted to ask you about," Maddy eased into the topic at hand. "I found an appliqué quilt in Helga's old room, a coverlet consisting of 15 blocks, each one depicting a silhouette of a woman. They appear to have been copied from old magazines."

"Oh, that old thing."

"You remember seeing it when you visited there as a child?" Lizzie couldn't contain her excitement.

"No, years later. She was nearly 20, as I recall. By then, she and I visited back and forth. We'd formed a bond, of sorts. I think hanging out with me was a respite from the constant company of her siblings. They never really liked each other all that much. Almost like they were strangers rather than family."

"How did Helga come to have the quilt?" asked Maddy. Looking for the provenance.

"She made it."

Cookie frowned, as if something didn't add up. "That can't be right. The quilt has a date stitched on it – 1925. Helga Hoople wasn't even born yet."

"Oh, that. We laughed over the date. Helga was extremely dyslexic. Always reversing letters and numbers. As a result of that affliction, she could barely read or write. She'd meant to stitch 1952, the year she made the quilt. Didn't even know she'd got it backward till I pointed it out."

You could see Lizzie's disappointment, like air released from a balloon. With the anachronistic Amelia Earhart picture and the reversed date, her belief that the quilt predated the famous Godey's Quilt was totally dashed.

"You're saying the 1925 was just a mistake?" Bootsie said. Trying to understand the mix-up.

"That's right. Helga was going to pull out the stitching and correct the date, but she never got around to it. She had started doing macramé. I think that appliqué was the only quilt she ever made. Too bad. She was pretty good at it."

1952 – that explained the Amelia Earhart illustration. She was already famous by then, having been the first female pilot to fly solo across the Atlantic in May of 1932. The quilt was made 20 years later!

Lizzie asked, "Where did she get the design for the quilt?"

Having been cooped up for weeks in rehab, Rita was in a talkative mood. "She saw a quilt in a magazine that she tried to copy. Dug out a lot of old magazines looking for pictures to use. I helped her cut them out and trace them. But she did all the sewing and appliquéing."

"And what happened to the quilt?" Maddy asked.

"I thought you said you found it."

"I did. But I'm curious what she did with it back then after moving on to macramé."

"Oh, she put it on her bed. Looked real nice. But I spilled a chocolate soda on it, so her mother packed it away and banished me from the Mansion."

"Banished you?"

"Kicked me out. Helga was quite upset with her mother. You'd think a young woman almost in her 20s could have any visitor she wanted, but Henrietta Hoople treated the quads like they were chattel. And maybe that's what they were. The Hoople Quadruples were a big moneymaker, my dad said. He booked their commercial appearances till he died of a heart attack in November, 1963. Same day John F. Kennedy was assassinated. He saw it on TV and immediately dropped dead. The shock of it, I suppose."

"Did you ever go back to the Hoople Mansion after that?"

"No. But when I came back from Chicago, Helga and I renewed our acquaintance. Her mother was dead by them – nobody left but the quads. Helga and I would get together for coffee at that little diner on South Main Street."

"Her mother's reaction over your spilling a chocolate shake on that quilt seems pretty harsh," commented Bootsie.

"I thought so too. But I don't think she ever truly approved of the quads playing with the help. That's how she and Henry looked on me and my dad. Other than the tutor, the kids were supposed to treat the servants like they were invisible."

"That's terrible."

"Yes, but Henrietta had a few screws loose – and I don't mean in her hip. By then she was coming unhinged. Henry had died. The demand for the quads was fading. She was frantic over money. Not that the Hooples needed any. They were already the richest folks in town."

"Did all their money come from the quadruples?" asked Lizzie. As a banker's wife, she was always curious about the financial angle.

"No, no," Rita shook her head, the bristly white hair swaying. "Henry Hoople was some kind of pharmaceutical millionaire. Invented a zit cream, as I recall. But he and Henrietta wanted more, so they used their children like a traveling circus, charging admission to see the fabulous quadruplets. As if they were freaks of nature. It was awfully hard on Helga, I can tell you that."

"It sounds like a horrible existence," said Maddy.

"Henry Hoople hired my dad to maximize their commercial value. He had been a talent booker for a radio station before that. Henry and Henrietta were an avaricious pair. Their goal was to sock away a billion dollars, my dad used to say. I don't think they ever made it, but I'll bet they came close." Rita Rutaberger paused as if she'd just heard her own words. "Of course, you'd know all about that, Maddy Madison – now that you've been inducted into the Hoople family."

"Not really," Maddy protested, but that didn't stop Rita.

"Those Hooples were richer than King Croesus," the woman commented as she pressed the buzzer for a nurse to bring her more water. Talking had made her thirsty.

~ ~ ~

Rita Rutaberger continued with her story, like a faucet that couldn't be turned off. "I took a job in Chicago with the Data Processing Division of IBM. Worked on the System/360 mainframe. Got married, stayed there until I took my retirement in 1980. I was a widow by then, so I came back home. No place else to go. Helga was still here, living in the Mansion, never married. She and I picked up our acquaintance, met for coffee at Cozy Café or sometimes the Pizza Hut. I refused to go back to the Mansion. Henrietta had hurt my feelings, treating me like I was beneath them. But I'd always liked Helga. Unfortunately, she had changed, got kinda ... crazy, there I said it. Maybe she got it from her mother. Or maybe life was simply getting the better of her."

"In what way?" queried Cookie.

"Floyd Hankins had dumped her, broke her heart. She never got over it. Started letting herself go, talking to herself, wandering around town. That was when I was in Chicago. When I came back we'd get together for coffee, but she wasn't really interested in hearing about my life. She only wanted to bemoan her fate – being a side show attraction, living an isolated existence, getting abandoned by Floyd."

"Why didn't it work out with Floyd?" asked Lizzie. She thrived on gossip like a baby on Similac. She was hooked on broken-hearts stories.

"Helga blamed herself, believed that she was wanting in some way. She had no self-confidence. Being one of four identical siblings, she felt that she had no personality of her own."

"That's quite sad."

"Yes, but I always suspected there was another reason Floyd broke up with her. I think Henrietta Hoople bought him off, paid him to go away. Don't know if it's true, but Floyd did come into some money about then. Purchased that house up near Gruesome Gorge State Park, eventually married one of the Baumgartner girls. Helga never got over it. Mark my word, that's why she jumped in the geyser and killed herself."

"When was the very last time you saw Helga Hoople?" asked Cookie, fitting the timeline into her head like loading an app onto a smart phone.

"The day before she disappeared. We had coffee. Thinking back on it, she may have been saying goodbye. I'll never forget when I heard Jebediah Crackleton had found her purse near the Blow Hole. At first, people suspected he'd killed her and tossed her into that bottomless pit. But none of the money was missing from her wallet so people eventually accepted that she'd committed suicide. She'd been acting weird for quite a while. Secretive, moping about. Next thing you know, she disappears down the Blow Hole. You probably remember that, Bootsie Purdue. Your husband was the top cop on that investigation."

"How long had it been since Floyd broke up with her?"

asked Cookie. Still working on the timeline.

"Maybe ten years before. Her mother died not long after that. Her father had passed away a few years earlier. That left the quads on their own. Hilda was reclusive, not going out in public. Herbie had moved to that little cottage on the river, breaking his ties with the family. And Helena was locked away in the booby hatch. I think I was Helga's only friend ... if you could call us that. We did have a long history, going all way back to childhood."

"It didn't bother her that you were 2 or 3 years younger?" asked Lizzie. Always age conscious.

"Not really," responded Rita. "The quads were socially stunted. They had led sophisticated lives, traveled, met famous people. But they were like bugs captured in amber, never being allowed to grow up. Like Peter Pan's Lost Boys."

Chapter Thirty-Two

Painting

Now that Beau Madison was retired, he took up a hobby. Aside from the fishing excursions with his pal Edgar Ridenour, he tried his hand at painting. Not houses, pictures. He wasn't very good but he was improving.

First, he did watercolors, but the results were too pastel for his taste. And then he worked with acrylics, but the look didn't have the seriousness he was aspiring for. That's how he settled on oils.

A trip to Victory's Art & Archery Supplies in Burpyville stocked him up on stretched canvas, a French easel, wooden palette with a thumbhole, an assortment of red sable brushes, and a studio set of .7 oz. tubes of Grumbacher pre-tested professional oils. Enough to give Rembrandt a run for his money, Beau told himself.

He started out painting still lifes: fruits and flowers and vases, the usual items. Then he tried a landscape or two, but felt silly sitting out in the open with a paintbrush and easel. So he wound up copying some of the old oil paintings scattered throughout the mansion.

He found a spare room in the Madison wing to serve as his studio. It had a window with north lighting.

Gathering up a selection of ancient oil paintings in gilded frames, he attempted to copy the brushstrokes of each painting, emulating the techniques of the various masters. He used the word "masters" loosely, for most of the paintings were by artists that he'd never heard of.

Maybe next he'd try portraits. Or dabble with abstract-expressionism. Or paint lily pads.

Beau found that painting relaxed him, cleared his head, helped him think. Today, as he worked on a chiaroscuro in the Dutch style, he couldn't help but reflect on the death of Boyd Aitkens. Opening the wrong bottle had likely led to his demise in Justin Harribald's meth lab. That stuff exploded so easily, he'd heard. But the question remained, what was Boyd doing there?

Making a purchase? No, Boyd Aitkens wasn't the druggie type. He liked Jim Beam Single Barrel Bourbon Whiskey much better.

Dropping by for social purposes? So far no one had suggested the two men even knew each other.

A business meeting? Hard to have a meeting with Mr. Harribald off shopping at the Food Lion. And what business would a wealthy watermelon farmer have with a living-on-the-edge drug manufacturer?

Financing him?

That gave Beau pause. Could Boyd Aitkens have been investing in a drug operation?

Naw, that didn't make sense.

~ ~ ~

Ben Bentley found it a challenge living with his wife Cookie. With her freak memory, it was hard to get away with anything. She could remember stray comments he made five years ago. Or the most minute detail that he'd overlooked on his Honey-Do list. She didn't forget.

Not that Ben had much to hide. He was a retired farmer who served as head of the Sons of Anthony Wayne, a statewide camper organization. And he was on the board of Haney Bros. Zoo and Exotic Animal Refuge. He'd donated the land for this popular local attraction. He'd inherited nearly a third of the county from his parents, Elijah and Elinor Bentley. They had become land barons by buying up unpaid tax claims.

Ben was a squat, broad-shouldered man, mindful of a character from Tolkien's *Lord of the Rings*. You could imagine him with a sword and shield, a warrior dwarf like Gimli, taking on the hordes of Elves. He'd been a high school wrestling champion and still displayed the musculature suited for pinning wiry opponents.

Ben had been amazed to learn of his wife's memory gift. But he was proud of her. Even if her knack of never forgetting kept him on his toes.

~ ~ ~

Gift? Sometimes Katherine "Cookie" Bentley felt it was a curse.

Nonetheless, this "affliction" sometimes came in handy. She focused her memory on the study of the inhabitants of Crackleton Crossing conducted in 2004 by the Geographical Society of Baltimore. The volume containing its findings – inbreeding, genetic defects, criminality, idiocy – had been subjected to a book burning by the locals, but the Caruthers Corners Historical Society had salvaged one pristine copy.

But there had been a supplemental report published along with the study, an appendix of genealogical charts. That was rarer to come by. Cookie didn't have a copy, but once she'd got a chance to thumb through one. That was enough to do the trick.

Cookie had her own genealogy charts at the Perricock Museum of Science & History, but they were far less complete than the Baltimore study. The Society had sent in a team of researchers who examined birth certificates, family Bibles, interviewed numerous family members, and conducted DNA tests. Pretty thorough by any standard.

She could picture the pages devoted to Sarah Celine Crackleton (née Jinks). The DNA results had confirmed that each of her known children – Jebediah, Claude, and Faith Ann – came from different fathers. None of them had been Happy Howard Crackleton.

Yet there were genetic problems with the fathers: Jeb was a giant with a dwarf for a son. Claude was mentally incapacitated. Faith Ann's kids had multiple afflictions (Gus had webbed toes).

However, it wasn't this list of infirmities that she was searching for in her mental filing cabinet. Ah, there it was! The name of the laboratory that conducted the DNA testing: Maryland Biological Analytics, Inc.

No doubt, they still had records of the DNA markers for residents of Crackleton Crossing. And she had a few strands of silver hair that had belonged to Madelyn Agnes Taylor Hoople Madison.

Katherine "Cookie" Bentley was determined to fill in the blanks on the Caruthers Corners Historical Society's genealogy charts.

Chapter Thirty-Three

Vivarium

Maddy couldn't keep putting it off, she told herself. Sooner or later, she'd have to go up to Crackleton Crossing and confront her "new" grandmother. Granny Crackleton was a legend in the county, an old witch woman who sat on her front porch, rocking and drinking Big Red soda and talking to travelers who had lost their way. Nobody deliberately went to the Crossing.

Beau nudged her that night as they watched a Netflix rerun of Disney's *Frozen*. Beau and N'yen had opted for a cable special on fly fishing, but as usual Maddy and Aggie won out. Somehow their vote carried more weight than did the others. "Go see the ol' crone," he urged. "You know you won't rest until you've done it."

"I'm not sure what I should do," she replied. "This is like finding out you're related to Charles Manson."

"Granny Crackleton's not quite that bad," he insisted. "At least I don't think so."

Tilly and Mark weren't there to weigh in, having gone to a concert at the Town Square and taking the little kids with them. They were meeting Tilly's brother Freddie and his family to hear a live performance by Paul Whittaker and His Hoosier Hotshots.

"I'll go with you, Grammy," volunteered Aggie. "After

all, she's my great-grandmother."

"Great-*great*-grandmother," corrected N'yen. "You left out one."

"That's amazing," said Maddy. "Five generations. Makes me feel old."

"You don't have to feel that way, Grammy," said N'yen, patting her hand, "You're the middle generation of the five. Granny Crackleton is the outlier."

"Thanks," she muttered. But it wasn't clear she meant it.

"I've met Granny Crackleton before," said Aggie. "She doesn't scare me."

"Me either," echoed the Asian boy. "I'm not afraid of a *mu... phu thuy*."

"A what?" said his grandfather. He looked up from the 55-inch Samsung LED Q7F 2160p Smart UHD TV. A new acquisition following the tornado. He pressed the pause button and *Frozen* was frozen on the screen.

"A witch," said N'yen. "There are witches in Vietnam too, particularly in the Ruc Lan Valley."

"How would you know?" Aggie berated her cousin. "You've never even been to Vietnam. You were born in Chicago."

"There are witches in Chicago too," the boy countered. "They gather at witch stores."

"Witch stores? Give me a break," she rolled her eyes.

"There are plenty of witch stores in Chicago – like Alchemy Arts, the Occult Bookstore, or Augustine's Spiritual Boutique."

"How do you know about such stores?" queried his grandmother, a worried expression creeping across her countenance.

"I looked them up on Atlas Obscura."

"Forget about witches," responded Aggie, clearly exasperated. "Granny Crackleton doesn't have any special powers, unless it's longevity. She's 99-years-old, for gosh sakes."

"Okay, okay," sighed Maddy. "Watch the movie. We'll go up to Crackleton Crossing first thing in the morning."

~ ~ ~

Off in a separate wing, N'yen could keep his own hours. No one to monitor him. So he climbed the stairs to the gable that capped his part of the mansion where his Celestron AstroMaster telescope was waiting on its sturdy tubular tripod. Adjusting the optics, he rotated the telescope to survey the town. The panoramic sweep revealed nothing out of the ordinary. A sleepy little town past its bedtime.

Down below the Fire Department was as bright as the Town Hall was dark. The concert at the park was over and everything had been shut down, even the sparkling lights on the bandstand. The street lights traced the grid of the town, with a dark zigzag marking the path of the recent twister.

Rebuilding took time, with some neighborhoods still showing scars of the storm. But houses were going up one after another, construction stimulated by the infusion of money from the Caruthers Corners Restoration Coalition along with some generous state and federal grants.

Shifting the telescope's view, N'yen examined the hills and dells of Pleasant Glade, the town's main cemetery. There was the caretaker's cottage, looking as if it could use a little care. He could see its sagging shutters and the peaked roof with missing shingles. No lights shone in its windows, understandable with Jasper Beanie still in the pokey. A liver-damaged alcoholic, he often slept it off in one of the holding cells at the police department.

Every now and then N'yen would see the red blink of a taillight, an accidental foot on the brakes in the parked cars of randy high schoolers. He knew Aggie and Bobby sometimes went there. He had spotted the boy's little Fiat Punta in the older section of the cemetery from time to time. He had a night scope, binoculars that worked on infrared. He couldn't make out any details, but he knew what went on in those cars parked in the cemetery. *Tsk, tsk!*

N'yen didn't think of himself as a voyeur, watching the town from above, looking in lighted windows, examining the cars parking in the cemetery. He thought of himself more like a sociologist. From up here atop Hoople Hill it was akin to studying an ant colony. He'd once had an Uncle Milton's Ant Farm, an educational toy that was the dry-land version of an aquarium. The proper word was *vivarium*, an enclosure for keeping animals under semi-natural conditions for observation or study.

That's what the citizenry of Caruthers Corners was to him – ants for observation. The town below the equivalent to Uncle Milton's Ant Farm. He wondered if he should write an algorithm to predict the movements of the insects below. Or study them for a Ph.D. dissertation.

Chapter Thirty-Four

Granny Crackleton

On Saturday morning Maddy drove her new Lincoln Navigator up to Crackleton Crossing, with Aggie and N'yen buckled up in the middle row of the seating. The gigantic three-ton vehicle with its twin-turbocharged 3.5-liter V-6 still managed to be nimble, even with its all-wheel drive. She had personally picked out the color she wanted, the Ivory Pearl Metallic TriCoat. The Navigator's 16 MPG wasn't great, but the car was really roomy, an 8-seater, big enough to hold all the Quilters Club – plus kids – without feeling crowded.

They found Granny Crackleton sitting in her usual spot in a rocker on the front porch of her little clapboard house near the crossroads. She was drinking a bottle of Big Red despite the early hour. Her version of breakfast. Approaching the century mark, she had no worries about contracting Diabetes Type 2 or hyperglycemia. At this age, death was her friend.

"Hello there, Maddy Madison," the old woman greeted her visitor from the porch. "I see you got yourself a new ride."

"Yes, my last one got blown away by the tornado." She opened the door and stepped out of the Navigator onto the mushy ground. It had been a rainy week. The pit of her stomach felt like she'd swallowed a can of Drano. Facing the old woman was not easy, knowing their newly revealed relationship. She'd rather be related to Osama bin Laden or Idi Amin.

"And looky – there's the kids in the backseat – that smart-mouthed little blonde and the Chinese boy."

"N'yen is Vietnamese."

"Same thing," shrugged the old woman. "A slant-eye is a slant-eye."

"And Aggie is not smart-mouthed. She merely speaks her mind."

"Same difference," said the old woman.

By now the kids were out of the car. Aggie planted her hands on her hips, obviously offended by the words. "If I'm defiant, maybe I take after you," she said.

"After me?"

"That's right. After all, you're my grandmother, several greats removed."

"I'd say most of her greats have been removed," muttered N'yen. Unimpressed by this garrulous old crank.

The elderly woman sat up in her rocking chair. "Everybody calls me Granny," she sputtered.

"That's because you Crackletons are so interbred you're really everybody's grandma," retorted the boy. He wasn't usually so rude to adults, but she had dissed his cousin Aggie. That was like putting Baby in a corner.

The old woman fixed him with a rheumy eye. "What do you know about us Crackletons, little man?"

"I read. The Baltimore study said you're all freaks."

"That study was slanderous," she spat.

"But accurate."

Granny Crackleton leaned forward. "Then you better be glad you're not related to us."

"I'm adopted, but Aggie is your direct descendant."

"Now how could that be?"

"We found the adoption papers," interjected Maddy. "That baby you gave away back in 1933 turned out to be Howard Hoople. He happens to be my biological father. And Aggie, of course, is my granddaughter ... just like I'm yours."

"Do tell now. I always wondered where that little baby boy wound up."

"Well, now you know."

"Hold on now, how can that be? Howard Hoople was one of them quadruplets. I only birthed one baby at a time – that one, then Jebediah, Claude, and Faith Ann."

"The quadruples were fake," blurted Aggie. "Four separate children passed off as brother and sisters."

"Ha! Now ain't that a joke on everyone. And folks say we Crackletons are crooks. Henry and Henrietta Hoople pulled off a big con job and got away with it."

"Til now."

"You gonna out 'em?" asked the old woman.

"Eventually. But I'll wait until Aunt Hilda is gone."

"What about Helga?"

Maddy cocked her head. "Aunt Helga is dead. She jumped in the geyser at Gruesome Gorge."

"That's what you think. My son Jeb was the one who reported her death. But everybody knows he's a liar. All us Crackletons are."

"You're saying your son Jebediah lied about Helga jumping into the Blow Hole? Are you saying he pushed her?"

"Ask him. According to you, he's your uncle.

Maddy sighed. "Apparently, that's true."

The old woman said, "A pox on you. You and your Quilters Club pals put him and his three sons – your cousins – in prison. Bet you're proud of that, treating your own flesh and blood like criminals."

"They *are* criminals," said Maddy.

"This is a very interesting family," said N'yen with a wide smile.

Chapter Thirty-Five

The Disappearance

Maddy couldn't get anything else out of Granny Crackleton. "Welcome to the family," the old woman spat, then hobbled into the rundown wooden house and firmly shut the front door with a bang. Leaving Maddy and her grandchildren standing there in the muddy front yard.

"Well, that was rude," said Aggie.

"Come along," coaxed Maddy. "Let's go over to the convenience store and I'll treat you to a Triple XXX."

"Oh boy," smiled N'yen. He was fond of root beer. "I'm glad I came along."

The cinderblock building sat cattycorner across the street, taking up one corner of the crossroad. The overpriced mini-mart was owned by Jebediah Crackleton, but currently it was being run by his sister Faith Ann while he was doing his jail time.

The interior of the store was crammed with shelves of off-brand canned goods, cellophaned sugar snacks, auto supplies, candy bars, chewing gum, and the like. Refrigerated coolers lined the righthand wall, the frosted glass hinting at soda pop, bottled water, and cartons of ice-cold beer. Carmel-colored bottles of Triple XXX stood like a formation of soldiers on the third shelf up on the far left.

Aggie and N'yen made a straight-line to the root beer.

Maddy stopped at the counter to converse with Faith Ann Ritchie. Maddy's friend Cookie was fostering one of Faith Ann's snot-nosed offspring, Augustus by name. How many other children Faith Ann had was not clear. But it was agreed each had a different daddy, none of them being Walter Ritchie, her first husband.

"Faith Ann, how did you get that shiner?" Maddy was taken aback by the woman's discolored face.

"Fell in the bathtub."

Somehow, Maddy sensed she was lying.

"I've got some interesting news for you," announced Maddy, pulling out the money to pay for the root beers.

"Nothing wrong with Gus, I hope. I'm not prepared to take him back. I'm busy here at the store. Business has picked up considerably now that Jeb is in jail. People ain't afraid to come here. Guess I got you to thank for that."

"Gus is fine. And your brother Jeb is a criminal who deserves to be behind bars."

"So what's your big news?" She handed Maddy change from the $20.

"I've just discovered that my biological father was your long-lost brother. That makes you my aunt."

"Do tell," shrugged Faith Ann. The Crackleton clan was so interbred that designations such as "aunt" or "uncle" were meaningless. "Cuz" covered most relationships.

"Thought you might like to know. I can't say I'm very excited by the circumstance."

"Who is this so-called long-lost brother of mine. Last I heard you were claiming Howard Hoople as your true daddy."

"He still is. Turns out, Howard's your brother. Your

mother gave him up for adoption years before you were born."

"Could be. Me, Jed, and Claude all had different daddies –although Happy Howard Crackleton claimed us all. If what you say about Howard Hoople is true, I s'pect he was named after ol' Happy Howard."

"I don't know about that. Facts are still coming out. Henry and Henrietta Hoople kept it a secret, claiming all four of the kids were quadruplets. I don't think your mother knew who adopted her baby. She was only 14 at the time."

"Long time ago. The ol' hag turned 99 a few months back. You'd think she's never gonna die. I can't take her demands much longer. I wish the Lord would just take her."

Maddy took a step back, shocked by the woman's tone. "That's no way to talk about your mother."

"More you get to know her, the more you'll be talking that way too. She's a trial, let me tell you that. Rings a little bell on a string and I gotta drop everything I'm doing and run across the street to bring her a Big Red. She surely has a sweet tooth – not that she's got any teeth left. Probably rotted out from all the sugar in them soda pops."

"Granny was telling me about your brother Jeb reporting Helga Hoople's falling in that geyser at Gruesome Gorge State Park. You know anything about that?"

"Word was she jumped."

"The way Granny told it, there seemed to be some doubt. Did Jeb kill her?"

Faith Ann scrunched up her face, as if trying to decide how much to say. "Don't know much about what actually happened. But Jeb said something about her paying him to make sure nobody ever saw her again."

PART III

Wendy was grown up. You need not be sorry for her. She was one of the kind that likes to grow up. In the end she grew up of her own free will a day quicker than other girls.

- *Peter Pan*, J.M. Barrie

Chapter Thirty-Six

Playing Catch Up

The next day was Tuesday, so the Quilters Club met for their weekly sewing bee at the Hoople Quilting Heritage Museum. Aggie was in school, and N'yen was off fishing with Beau and Edgar Ridenour. The boy's parents would be coming down to pick him up tomorrow. They had just returned from their seminar in Colorado, all invigorated and ready to apply new techniques to the youth center they ran in Chicago.

Maddy stopped by Cozy Café to pick up four to-go cups of steaming Maxwell House coffee and a dozen freshly-made doughnuts – three each. Her treat.

Bootsie would talk Lizzie out of one of her doughnuts. Some things were predictable. Lizzie ate like a parakeet; Bootsie like a goose being readied for Thanksgiving.

By the time Maddy arrived, she'd already finished off one of her doughnuts, coconut sprinkles with a crème filling. Tasty, in spite of the 350 calories.

Lizzie had tidied up the sewing room since last week's gathering. Quilt quarters and stray fabrics had been packed away in the cubbyholes that lined the far wall. Textile scraps stuffed in a barrel in the corner. Lizzie had a big red smile on her face. She was always in a good mood when her husband was off fishing with Beau Madison – as if relieved from babysitting duties with a 60-year-old child. Edgar had become quite the slacker after retiring from his position as president of the local bank. He and Beau fished three days a week.

Cookie was late, having had a meeting with Gus's teacher. He was acting up again, an unruly child who defied authority. Genetics asserting itself, she feared. But that wasn't a subject to have with her friend Maddy – the Crackleton bloodline being a sore subject at the moment.

Bootsie was sitting there like a female Buddha, a beneficent smile on her chubby face. She obviously had news and wasn't about to give it out until everybody was seated in their place. Lizzie was about to pee herself with anticipation. Cookie fanned herself and said, "Get on with it." Maddy cocked her head with interest as she handed out the doughnuts and coffee.

"I heard from a reliable source –" Bootsie began.

"– your husband Jim, you mean," interjected Cookie.

"– that Justin Harribald is turning state's evidence against Salvatore Milano."

"Sal the Whisperer?" gasped Maddy. "What's he got to do with Mr. Harribald's meth lab?" She was familiar with the Indy mob boss through Barnabas Soltairé, administer of the Hoople Quadruplets Trust Fund. Barnabas used to be Sal Milano's lawyer, a disreputable history of fronting for the Mafia that he didn't bother to deny.

"You didn't think Mr. Harribald manufactured that crystal meth for his own use, did you?" Bootsie replied. "He supplied it for Salvatore Milano's distribution chain. The Mob has hundreds of dealers on the street in Indy, Jim says."

"N-methylamphetamine costs about $7 per gram to make," explained Cookie, drawing on her super-dooper memory. "It is then diluted and sold on the street for about $100 per gram in the Northeast and Midwest. A nice markup, but of course the distributor – the Mob – gets a lion's share of the money."

"Selling drugs is like Amway," observed Bootsie. "The guys at the bottom make nothing, the guys at the top make a great deal."

"Salvatore Milano won't be happy about Mr. Harribald flipping on him," observed Lizzie. "People who rat on the Mob have a habit of turning up dead." She read a lot of crime novels, Elmore Leonard and Jeffery Deaver, sometimes James Ellroy.

"Oh my heavens, poor Justin," exclaimed Cookie. Reminding everyone that she used to be Mr. Harribald's "teacher's pet" back in high school.

"There, there," soothed Maddy. "The FBI will see that he's protected."

"That's right," confirmed Bootsie. "Jim says Mr. Harribald will probably be granted immunity and hidden away in a Federal Witness Protection Program."

"We won't have to worry about ol' Justin," said Lizzie, rolling her eyes. "He'll probably wind up in a Florida retirement home with a fat monthly allowance. He'll be chasing nurse's aides down the beach in his underwear."

"No murder charge?" asked Cookie. Referring to the death of Boyd Aitkens in the lab explosion.

"Jim says no charges are being filed on that," replied Bootsie. "Boyd was his business partner. And he was in the lab of his own free will when it exploded. In fact, the explosion was probably Boyd's fault, him messing with the equipment."

"I don't understand why Boyd would get involved with manufacturing meth," said Lizzie. "He was already filthy rich. Owned the biggest watermelon farm in the entire county."

Bootsie had the answer. "Jim says the Feds told him that Salvatore Milano backed Boyd's buying up all that land. So the meth was a way of paying Milano back. He was laundering Mob drug money through his farm."

"How do the Feds know this?" asked Maddy, spreading out her quilting material on the large table. "That sounds like insider information."

"It is. The boy who acted as runner between the meth lab and the Mob confessed."

"Who was that?" pressed Lizzie. "Do I know him?" Always hungry for gossip.

"I'm not supposed to say. The kid is underaged. But it was Teddy DiMacchio."

Maddy's mouth dropped open. "Teddy D? He and Prissy Moretz double-date with Aggie and Bobby Elwood."

"Don't worry," Bootsie reassured her. "Teddy D isn't a street dealer selling crystal meth – or hot ice or chalk dust or whatever else they call it these days – to other kids. He was just a delivery boy. That's how he afforded to buy that nice car."

"A very *nice* car," agreed Lizzie. Teddy DiMacchio had recently bought the Infiniti QX60. Loaded, with all-wheel drive, a 295-hp V6 engine, Bose® sound system, and custom leather interior. Cool to the nth degree.

"Hmm. That *is* a pretty pricey automobile for a high

school student, now that you think of it," muttered Maddy. There would be no more double dating for her granddaughter. She'd speak to Tilly about it.

Bootsie waved her friend's concerns away. "Don't worry, Teddy D won't be needing that fancy car for future dates. He'll likely do some jail time, Jim says. He'll be dating a prisoner called Bubba who shares the cell with him. His car will be auctioned off."

"Teddy D's not going to be happy about that," commented Maddy. "He loved that car more than he loved Prissy."

"And Prissy loved that car more than she loved Teddy D," countered Lizzie, suppressing a smile.

"Do you think Teddy D can cut himself a deal?" asked Maddy.

Bootsie shrugged. "Depends on what he's got to trade. My guess is Mr. Harribald gave them everything they wanted. First to flip, first out the door. Teddy D could be left holding the bag."

"Holy moly, I can't believe there was a mob-backed meth lab right across the street from the quilting museum," said Lizzie. She sounded bemused, as if this were somehow a claim to fame. Like the museum was one of the stops on a Hollywood star map.

"And I can't believe Justin Harribald was the one running it," sighed Cookie. She was looking a little teary. A wave of nostalgia and all that. Apparently, she'd really had a thing for her old teacher.

"There, there," Maddy patted her girlfriend on the shoulder. "He simply got old and desperate. Teachers' pensions are not very generous, it's sad to say."

"Don't worry about Mr. Harribald," said Bootsie. "He'll make out like a bandit in a Witness Protection Program." The emphasis had been on the word *bandit*.

"Hard to believe, Boyd Aitkens dead, Justin Harribald in jail, and Tommy D working as a courier for the Mob. How did our little town become so embroiled in criminal activities?" Cookie shook her head in disbelief. Rearranging the town's history in her mind.

~ ~ ~

"On another matter," Maddy Madison deliberately changed the topic, "I went up to Crackleton Crossing over the weekend to visit my 'new' grandmother."

"How did that go?" asked Cookie.

"Well, I think. That is to say, she couldn't have cared less."

"I take it there'll be no family gathering at Thanksgiving," said Bootsie. Sarcasm dripping from her words like honey glaze on a roast turkey. The holiday was coming up week after next – fourth Thursday of November.

"Who would want to share a turkey with those turkeys anyway?" declared Lizzie.

"Hey, those are my relatives you're talking about," Maddy pointed out.

"Gus's relatives too," Cookie spoke up. She was very protective of her foster son, a Crackleton right down to his webbed toes.

"Sorry," Lizzie retracted her statement. "Sometimes I can't help myself. Granny Crackleton spooks me. She should be peddling apples to Snow White."

Maddy halfway smiled. "Yes, I admit Granny Crackleton's an unsavory character. But there's no doubt that she's my fraternal grandmother. You've all seen the birth certificate."

"Did the adoption papers tell you anything more?" asked Bootsie.

"We haven't found those yet. The Hoople Mansion is like a warehouse for over a century's worth of junk. We've been searching high and low for further documentation, but no luck. Most of the important records were in a safe in the basement."

"Basement?" said Bootsie. "It's more like a dungeon down there."

"Speaking of searching the Mansion, have you and Aggie turned up any other interesting quilts?" Lizzie wanted to know. She could be a little self-absorbed at times.

"No," Maddy shook her head, silver hair shimmering in the fluorescent light. Yesterday she'd paid a visit to Helen of Troy Spa and Beauty Salon. Margie Yost had given her a $50 perm and a pedicure. "The one I found seems to be Aunt Helga's only venture into quilt making. That's according to her old friend Rita."

Sadly, the truth about their "Frank Leslie" quilt's provenance had been disheartening. Lizzie was now referring to it as "the phony Godey Quilt." She had to find another exhibit to fill the slot she'd reserved for it in the museum's schedule.

Cookie continued, "Too bad about Helga Hoople taking her own life. Just because she got dumped by Floyd Hankins." Maybe she was thinking back to her own youthful fling with their history teacher. As it happened, she'd been pretty depressed when Mr. Harribald moved on to his next pet.

"There's something odd about Helga's suicide," said Maddy.

"Like what?" That got Lizzie's attention. Lurid details were like catnip for the redhead.

"Granny Crackleton – my grandmother, that is – hinted that there was something hinky about Helga's death. Remember, it was her son Jeb – my uncle, it turns out – who reported that Helga had jumped into that geyser. But no body was ever found."

Bootie's eyes bulged like Barbara Bush's. "Are you saying Helga Hoople is still alive?"

"No, no. That is, I don't know what I'm saying. Granny Crackleton's comments left me confused."

"Do you think she faked her own death?" asked Cookie.

"Or did Jeb Crackleton kill her?" Bootsie offered an alternative theory.

"Now that's an interesting thought," said Lizzie. "I wouldn't put it past him." She remembered how he'd once threatened them with a gun.

"He might have killed her for the money in her purse," speculated Cookie.

"There wasn't any money missing," Bootsie reminded them. She was more familiar with the case than the others, thanks to her husband's early-on involvement.

"I think there's something hinky about Aunt Helga's death," said Maddy.

"Technically, she's not your aunt," Cookie pointed out. "Since the quads weren't actually related, Helga wasn't your father's sister." She had already rearranged the Hoople genealogy chart in her head.

"No, they weren't related by birth," said Maddy. "But

they were all legally adopted. That makes her my aunt."

"Okay, I concede to your point."

"I wonder who were Helga's parents," said Lizzie. A look of determination on her thin, hawk-like face.

"Hmm," said Cookie. "Maybe in the course of the investigation we can find out where each of the Hoople Quadruples came from."

"That would require finding the adoption papers," said Bootsie.

"Maybe, maybe not," replied Lizzie. "As N'yen told us, sometimes names are changed on adoption papers."

"No, I think that happens with birth certificates being reissued," corrected Bootsie.

Maddy held up her hands like a policeman stopping traffic. "Girls, I think you're getting carried away. It's likely we'll never know the true families of the quadruplets."

But she was wrong about that.

Chapter Thirty-Seven

Date Night

N'yen typed IS A SAFE A VAULT? into his search engine and hit the return key. The answer appeared as smoothly as if he'd asked a Magic 8-Ball:

> **Vaults** and **Strongrooms**. The primary difference between a **safe,** a **vault**, and a **strongroom** is that safes are movable. Vaults and strongrooms are integral to the building they are located in. A vault is a secure room or series of rooms.

Hmm. That gave him something to consider. That note in the rosewood box had said SECRET PAPERS IN VAULT. But the Herring-Hall-Marvin safe in the basement had wheels. It was moveable. Was there a clue there?

He'd have to give it some more thought. He was determined to solve the mystery of the Secret Papers before his parents took him back to Chicago. He'd show his cousin Aggie that she'd have to get up early in the morning to out-sleuth him! He was a regular Charlie Chan.

Okay, so he was Vietnamese, not Chinese. But neither was Sidney Toler, the guy who played Charlie Chan in 22 movies!

~ ~ ~

Aggie got home at 11 o'clock on the dot – the deadline set by her dad for date nights.

"Hi, Grammy. What are you still doing up?"

197

"I got caught up watching the 10 O'clock News. They were covering the death of Boyd Aitkens."

"Was he really involved in that meth lab?" asked Aggie as she hung her coat in the hall closet. The weather was turning nippy. In the 40s. But it had quit raining.

Maddy yawned, not used to the late hour. "That's what they're saying. Hard to believe we know a drug lord."

"You know two of them. Didn't you say that old man who was making the drugs used to be your high school history teacher?"

"Both US History and World History."

"Actually we know three drug dealers, if what they're saying about Teddy D is true."

"Likely it is. Mr. Harribald turned him in."

"Squealed on him, you mean."

"Turned State's evidence is the proper term," corrected her grandmother.

"I should have been suspicious when Teddy D bought that new car – with his dad's business wiped out and him with no job. He had to get that money from somewhere – but running drugs?"

"I guess you never really know other people," Maddy said.

"Where's N'yen?"

"In his room. Probably building a cyclotron."

"That would be funny if it probably wasn't true," grinned Aggie.

"What did you see at the movies tonight?"

"Oh ... uh, Bobby and I saw *Fantastic Beasts*."

"I thought that movie came out a couple of years ago."

"That was *Fantastic Beasts and Where to Find Them*,"

she said hastily. "This is its sequel, *Fantastic Beasts: The Crimes of Grindelwald.*"

"Oh."

"Well, goodnight.

"Aggie, is that a hickey on your neck?"

The girl stopped, one foot on the stairs. "Uh, no. A mosquito bite."

"Sleep tight," said Maddy, knowing there were no mosquitos this time of year. She knew a "love bite" when she saw one. Maybe her granddaughter was growing up a little too fast.

~ ~ ~

There was more truth to that than Aggie would have been happy to admit. Lately, instead of going to the movies in Burpyville, she and Bobby Elwood had been parking in the cemetery. All the kids did it, especially the seniors. While Bobby and Aggie were only sophomores this year, they *were* officially going steady. That was called a "parking permit" at Caruthers High.

Jasper Beanie, the cemetery caretaker, had a longstanding arrangement with the local kids. He left the gate unlocked at night; in return they left an occasional pint of Wild Boar on the fencepost in front of his cottage. Like a tribute paid to a pagan god.

Nonetheless, most couples parked as far away from the caretaker's cottage as they could. Word was Jasper liked to peek into the windows of cars, catching necking couples unaware. The sneaky old pervert!

Aggie enjoyed these make-out sessions with Bobby. So far, she had successfully held him in check, restricting their activities to playing kissy-kissy, with a minimum of touchy-feely. He'd been a gentleman about it – mostly.

In bed that night Aggie thought about Bobby. She really liked him. She could even imagine them being married one day. But should she settle for the first (and only) guy she'd ever kissed. And what about college? She had a fund that would pay all her tuition. Maybe she'd better cool things down a bit with Bobby. No need to get carried away with young romance.

Chapter Thirty-Eight

Back to Chicago

Bill and Kathy Madison arrived that morning to take N'yen home. He had to get back to school – not that he'd fallen behind in his studies. Having read all the assigned textbooks, he was already ahead of his fellow classmates in the learning department. And that was after having skipped two grades. At this speed, he would be in college before Aggie graduated high school.

Truth is, Aggie was a pretty smart cookie herself – but nowhere near the genius level of her cousin. Although a straight-A student, she realized she'd never quite match N'yen's academic level. What grade average was there above an A+?

Despite their recent differences – N'yen resented the time she spent with Bobby Elwood – she was going to be sad to see him return to Chicago. She needed his gray cells to help her solve these mysteries of the Hoople family tree.

Two Family Secrets uncovered. How many more to go? It was anybody's guess.

Aggie was sure there were more documents to be found within the dusty recesses of the Hoople Mansion. She was convinced there was more going on here than a fraud to pass off four unrelated children as quadruplets.

~ ~ ~

"You've got to find the vault," said N'yen as he climbed into the backseat of his parents' high-mileage Subaru Forester. "That's where the adoption papers are."

Aggie looked puzzled. "The vault? We already found that – that big steel Herring-Hall-Marvin safe in the basement."

"Technically, a safe is not a vault. And that scrap of paper definitely said *vault*."

"Okay, Mr. Smarty Pants. What is a vault?"

"Look in the dictionary," he called out the window as the green station-wagon-based SUV pulled away to begin its four-hour trip back to Chicago, the trunk filled computers and telescopes and microscopes.

~ ~ ~

Aggie had to admit it was kinda lonely with N'yen gone. Sure, they had fought like Katzenjammer Kids this visit, but he was truly her best-est friend in the whole wide world. If he'd only get over his snit about Bobby Elwood. She shouldn't have to choose between her cousin and her boyfriend.

Late that afternoon Aggie wandered into the mansion's library. The walnut bookshelves lining three of the walls held thousands of leather-bound volumes – first editions and antiquities and rarities. In one corner stood a faded globe on a swivel stand – in effect, a 3-dimensional map of the world. In another corner she spotted a sturdy wooden podium that displayed a dictionary thicker than a New York phonebook.

That was the place to look, according to her cousin. So she thumbed through the big dictionary to the *V*'s in the very back. Tracing her finger down the page she came to the following listing:

> **vault**[1] | vôlt | *noun*
>   **1** a roof in the form of an arch or a series of
>   arches, typical of churches and other large,
>   formal buildings.
>   • *Literary* a thing resembling an arched roof,
>   especially the sky: *the vault of heaven.*
>   • *Anatomy* the arched roof of a cavity, especially
>   that of the skull: *the cranial vault.*
>
>   **2** a large room or chamber used for storage,
>   especially an underground one.
>   • a secure room in a bank in which valuables
>   are stored.
>   • a chamber beneath a church or in a graveyard
>   used for burials.
>
> **vault**[2] | vôlt | *verb [no object]*
>   **1** leap or spring while supporting or propelling oneself
>   with one or both hands or with the help of a
>   pole: *he **vaulted over** the gate.*
>
>   **2** *noun* an act of vaulting.

She read the various definitions three times before giving up. "Well, that was not particularly helpful," she told herself. N'yen had told her to look in the dictionary. Probably his idea of a joke, sending her on an etymological wild goose chase. The little pinhead.

~ ~ ~

That night as she lay in bed, blonde hair spread across her pillow, Agnes thought of Bobby Elwood. He had such cute freckles across his nose. His eyes were the same sparkling green as a 7-Up bottle. He was such a good kisser.

N'yen was jealous of the time she spent with Bobby, but that was just too bad. Bobby was her boyfriend.

Maybe it worked both ways, she told herself. Sometimes Bobby seemed resentful of the time she spent with the Quilters Club. Did he object to her quilting ... or to the sleuthing. She and N'yen were pretty good at helping Grammy solve crimes.

As her mind wandered, she thought more about N'yen's departing words. "Look in the dictionary," he'd said. But all she'd found were multiple definitions for *vault*. That didn't help. Nonetheless, she felt sure that the little twerp had been giving her a clue. Had he already figured out where to find the Secret Papers? If so, why not just *tell* her!

Then it occurred to her, N'yen *didn't* know. He was just pointing her in the direction that he would've looked if he hadn't had to go home.

Okay, she would follow his coaxing. Give it some thought. Apply what her cousin called "subconscious cerebration." That is, she'd let it rattle around in the back of her head till an idea popped out.

Then she'd know where to look.

As she drifted off to sleep, she muttered, "Maybe in the morning ...."

Chapter Thirty-Nine
The Nudge

Edgar Ridenour was tolerant of his wife's hobbies. He had added a wing onto their house over near the river to hold her patchwork quilts. They had run out of friends and family to gift with these stacks of decorative coverlets. Everybody they knew had one (or two in some cases).

He was pleased when she got appointed executive director of the Hoople Quilting Heritage Museum. It got her out of the house. Up till then she had lounged around the house, watching soap operas and reality TV on their widescreen Panasonic, a 65-inch hi-res model. Somehow she remained skinny despite a steady diet of bon-bons and Godiva chocolate.

Edgar spent as much of his time as he could manage in the woods and on the river. This daily separation might well be the secret to their 40-year marriage's success.

His passion was fishing. He and his buddy Beau Madison practically lived on the waters of the Wabash. He particularly enjoyed when young N'yen joined them on their jaunts. Estranged from his own daughter, the boy was like a surrogate son.

Edgar had been shaken by Boyd Aitkens's death. The watermelon farmer had been the largest customer of the bank. They had become close friends when Edgar served as the bank's president. That camaraderie continued even after his retirement.

He was one of the few people who knew about Boyd's daughter. After Boyd's youngest son died, he turned his attention to Suzy Q. She was the apple of his eye.

The revelation that Ralph was not his biological son explained their distant relationship. Although Ralph functioned as foreman of Aitkens Produce, he might as well have been a hired hand.

"Our pal Jim seems convinced Boyd's death was an accident," noted Edgar. "I'm not so sure myself. Mixed up with drug dealers, Boyd may have gotten in over his head."

"You think so?" said Beau, casting his line to a shady spot near the abutment of the Highway 101 Bridge.

"My opinion doesn't count. Jim's the police chief. But I worry he's being a little hasty."

"Only way to get him to change his mind is show him some evidence."

"Got any?"

"No, but maybe the Quilters Club will turn up some."

"Are they looking into Boyd's death? Lizzie hasn't mentioned it."

Beau reeled in his line, to cast again, thinking he might be able to place his hook closer to the abutment. "I'm not sure. But maybe there's something we can do to nudge them along."

"Like what?"

"Call our little buddy."

~ ~ ~

"Granny, what's this business 'bout Maddy Madison claiming I'm her aunt." Faith Ann had walked across from the convenience store to deliver another Big Red soda pop.

"Could be true. Who knows for sure?"

"You mean to say Howard Hoople might've been my brother?"

"I gave away a li'l boy back then. It could've been him. I gave the baby to Rev. Dimpledorf. Don't know who he adopted it out to."

"If we was related to Howard Hoople, we should've cashed in on it," said Faith Ann. "Them Hooples are rich as the Rockefellers."

"Maybe not quite that rich," corrected the elderly woman. "But they got more money than I can count."

"Who was that baby's daddy – Happy Howard?"

"No, that was 'fore I met him. Hard to say who it was. I was pretty active when I was a teenager."

"You seemed to have stayed pretty active. I was a late-in-life baby."

"You ain't no different. Your boy Gus is only eight or nine."

"He's got a good home with them Bentleys. Ben Bentley owns a whole lot of land. That boy's set for life."

"If your brother turned out to be Howard Hoople, I'd say he fared A-Okay too."

"So who was his daddy?"

Granny Crackleton took a sip of the red cream soda. "Told you, I'm not sure."

"Take a guess."

"Could've been any number of suitors. Richard Purdue – that was N.L. Purdue's daddy, the one what started the E-Z Seat factory. Or Jimbo Martin – Jimbo's Big Boulder is named after him. Or Dirty Dean Winslow – he was quite the rascal. Died in prison. He cut a man's ear off with his Barlow knife."

"Who was my daddy?"

"Told you I'm not sure. But I think it was my cousin Rich. He was surely a handsome devil. I think you got his eyes."

Chapter Forty

Flipping

Justin Ford Harribald was transferred to Indianapolis, where he'd been remanded to FBI custody. He would be questioned, deposed, and forced to testify against Sal "the Whisperer" Milano, the mobster who distributed the crystal meth he produced. Then – and only then – he'd be whisked away into the Witness Protection Program, never to be seen again.

A new life. It wouldn't be fancy, he was told, but it would be a life. The alternative was a bullet in the head, courtesy of Sal the Whisperer's business associates.

Justin Harribald wished he'd never got mixed up with these criminals. But Boyd Aitkens approached him, offering a lot of money. Ten dollars a gram – that could be $1,000 profit on a good day. He needed the money. No, not gambling debts or a drug habit. He suffered from rheumatoid arthritis, his out-of-pocket cost for Enbrel running almost $50,000 a year. So much for Affordable Health Coverage.

He'd known Boyd Aitkens for 35 years, for that's how old Ralph was. Boyd's wife June – Ralph's mother – had been one of his pets. She'd got pregnant, the silly twit, but Boyd had stepped up and married her, raised the boy as his own. Problem solved.

Oddly, Justin Harribald and Boyd Aitkens had become friends after June died of pneumonia. It was as if they had her ghost in common, a connection that drew them together.

Working for Boyd had been good, in that it gave him a chance to get to know Ralph, the son he'd never acknowledged. He regretted their estrangement, knowing he'd missed the chance in life to be a true father. He should have married June himself, rather than leaving her to Boyd. He'd always kinda resented Boyd for taking that away from him – although he had to admit the man had treated Ralph well, raising him as his own.

But he'd come to know Ralph these past couple of years. In addition to being the foreman of Aitkens Produce, he'd been the go-between for the drug business. Boyd was too busy to get involved.

That had been Boyd Aitkens's biggest mistake, letting the father and son get to know each other.

~ ~ ~

Teddy D had one more surprise up his sleeve. He'd won points with the Feds by naming all the meth labs in Caruthers County. Flipping on his employers "like a pancake at IHOP," as Special Agent in Charge Neil Wannamaker had put it.

But in a routine interview with the FBI agents it came out that he'd once met Salvatore Milano.

"You actually met the Big Man?"

"Yeah, why?"

Needless to say, the agents were surprised. Sal the Whisperer didn't dirty his hands with street-level underlings. Kept his distance. Nobody to tie him to the dirty work. "What did Sal Milano look like?"

"Hard to say. I wasn't paying close attention. A little guy, mustache, slicked-back dark hair. Oh yeah, he had a little tuft of white hair on one side of his head. What's with that?"

The tuft of white hair was the capper, proof that he'd actually met Sal. "That's where he got shot by Madman Mike Nuncio. Bullet lodged in his brain. It's probably still in there. Hair came back white at the point of impact."

The other agent pressed him. "So how did you come to meet Sal?"

Teddy D shrugged, broad shoulders stretching against his tan T-shirt. "I was making a delivery in Indy when in walks Sal Milano. Came down to check on his men. I think he was worried they were shorting him."

"What did he say to you?"

"Just looked at me and said, 'Who the ka-doodle are you?' in that raspy voice of his. I said, 'I bring the crystal in from the labs,' and he said, 'Don't steal any of my dope ... I'm watching you.'"

"He actually said, 'My dope?'"

Teddy D looked from agent to agent. "Yeah, why?"

"You'll testify to that?"

"Sure. If that'll cut my sentence."

It would. Sal was a bigger fish.

~ ~ ~

Aggie thought more about the definitions for *vault*. The one that made the most sense to her was a *bank vault*.

Didn't the two words kinda go together?

There was only one bank in town – Caruthers Corners Savings & Loan. Uncle Edgar used to be its president. Aunt

Lizzie was the major stockholder. Her grandfather had founded the bank way back when.

But the adoption papers – she assumed those were the secret papers – wouldn't be lying inside the bank's main vault, where it kept its money on hand. But there were safe deposit boxes – those were part of the vault, weren't they?

She phoned Aunt Lizzie and explained her problem. "Could you check to see if there are any safe deposit boxes in the name of Hoople?"

Lizzie weighed the privacy issues in her head, then said what the heck, this was Aggie. "Back to you in a half hour," she said.

"Okay."

True to Lizzie's word, Aggie's iPhone buzzed precisely 30 minutes later. "Sorry, kiddo," said the redhead. "No boxes listed under Hoople. I guess they keep their valuables in that big fortress they call home."

"No, we've already looked top to bottom. Nothing in the safe. The adoption papers aren't there."

"Maybe Aunt Hilda destroyed them. Protecting the Family Secret, as she calls it." Maddy had shared the details of the phony quadruplets with the Quilters Club. They gals had few secrets from each other.

"Aunt Hilda says not."

"Dearie, the old girl has Parkinson's. She might not remember. Maddy says everything is getting pretty jumbled with her memory."

"That's true. But I think the secret papers – the adoption papers – are still hidden in some vault. I was sure they'd be in the bank's vault."

"Records show that none of the Hooples ever had an

account with the Savings & Loan. Their money is managed by a large bank in Indianapolis. You might try there.

"Fat chance of that," muttered Aggie. No bank would discuss its depositors with a 15-year-old girl.

"I just did."

"Yes, but you know me."

"Well, then. You could have your grandmother ask Barnabas Solaire. He manages the Hoople finances."

"No luck there. He told Grammy she had to find the papers herself. I think they will reveal Secret Number Three."

"Number Three? How many secrets does the Hoople family have?"

"Lots apparently. N'yen will be thrilled."

~ ~ ~

"Edgar and I miss our fishing buddy," Beau Madison said over the phone. "We didn't catch a thing today. Don't think that's ever happened before."

"Gee, Grampy, you guys must be losing your touch. There are plenty of cats to be had in the Wabash. What kinda bait were you using?"

"Chicken livers."

"Not my favorite," said N'yen. "But you should've caught something. Maybe a carpsucker or redhorse or a bluegill."

"Nope, not even a bluntnose minnow."

"That's sure unusual. The Wabash is considered the most diverse fishing stream in the US." The boy was a font of knowledge.

"Guess you're our lucky charm."

"Yeah, I must be."

"I've been thinking about poor ol' Boyd Aitkens getting blown to Kingdom Come. Some of it puzzles me."

"What's that, Grampa? Meth labs are dangerous. I saw the explosion. A big ball of fire."

"Can't help wondering what Boyd was doing there all by himself. Doesn't make sense. Teddy DiMacchio dropped him off, but Mr. Harribald wasn't even there. Boyd was all by himself in the lab."

"Maybe we'll never know."

"Maybe. But I wonder if there's any clue in his phone records or emails."

"Didn't Uncle Jim check them?"

"I worry your Uncle Jim was a little quick writing it off as an accident."

"You wanna find out who Mr. Aitkens talked with?"

"I'd be curious."

Chapter Forty-One

The Family Vault

That Friday night Aggie had a date with Bobby Elwood. Now that he had his own car – that banged-up, smoke-spewing '98 Fiat Punto – they didn't have to rely on double-dating with Teddy D and Prissy Moretz. Besides, Prissy's family had moved to Pitsville after the recent tornado, and Teddy D was in jail – could you believe that?

Aggie and Bobby were getting pretty serious. He had given her his class ring to wear around her neck on a gold chain. Their friends considered them an item. As if she were Bobby's property. Although a latent feminist at heart – Gloria Steinem was her idol – Aggie found that she didn't mind the designation. She liked the idea of being "Bobby's girl."

As usual, they skipped the movies and parked in the Pleasant Glade Cemetery for a make-out session. She was fascinated by this new element of sex in their relationship. Oh, nothing beyond second base – hands above the clothing. She was a "good girl" by all definitions. Nonetheless, she particularly liked – as Bobby awkwardly called it – swapping spit. Kissing was so coooool.

Because Pleasant Glade had a caretaker – that old sot, Jasper Beanie – they always parked in the Old Section of the cemetery, as far from the caretaker's cottage as you could get in the maze of narrow roads that wound their way among the tombstones. Down in this lower section near the river, there was virtually a village of above-ground crypts and granite-faced mausoleums. Kinda spooky if you stopped to think about it.

But tonight Aggie couldn't help but think about N'yen's advice to look in the dictionary. What was he trying to tell her? Was he deliberately playing mind games? Those definitions had been all over the place.

Vaulting could mean to run. Or a vault was part of a church's architecture. Or it was a secure room in a bank. Or even a burial chamber.

She had already phoned her Aunt Lizzie to ask if there were any safe deposit boxes in the name of Hoople at Caruthers Corners Savings & Loan. Elizabeth Ridenour being the largest stockholder in the hometown bank that her grandfather had founded, she could get the info if anyone could.

The answer had come back quickly. Nada.

So where else would she find a vault?

"What's the matter?" asked Bobby. "Why did you stop?"

Aggie sat up, adjusting her dress. "Nothing. I just thought of something."

"Can we talk about it later?" he said, leaning forward to kiss her again.

"No, wait. Let me think this through."

He paused to determine if she were serious. She was. He knew that look. "Okay, think about what?" he sighed, sitting back against the door.

"Something my cousin said about vaults."

"You mean bank vaults?"

"I thought so. But that didn't pan out."

"Then what kinda vault?"

"Look at that big stone structure over there." She pointed her index finger at a hulking shape just beyond the Fiat's right fender.

"A crypt. What about it?"

"Read the name on it."

"H-O-O-P ... HOOPLE. How about that! A family mausoleum."

"Exactly – a vault."

"Yeah, but what of it? We're surrounded by dozens of them."

She opened the car door. "Let's go see if we can get inside."

He blinked his eyes in the sudden glare of the overhead light. "Are you crazy? Break into a mausoleum filled with dead people. No way."

"C'mon. Help me and I'll let you put your hand inside my blouse."

"Honest?"

"Would I lie about a thing like that?"

Bobby grinned. "Let's kick that door in," he said.

Chapter Forty-Two

Night Caller

"Grammy, wake up!" Aggie said, shaking her grandmother's shoulder gently. It was only 10:47 p.m. but Maddy and Beau went to bed early – a Midwestern tradition of sorts. Especially for those 60 and older.

"Hmm, what?" Maddy rolled over to face the blonde intruder.

"Grammy, wake up," the girl repeated.

"Aggie? What on earth are you doing here in our bedroom this time of night? Is something wrong? Are your sisters all right?"

"Everybody's fine, but there's something you've gotta see."

"See? See what?" The silver-haired woman sat up in bed, wiping the sleep out of her eyes.

"I found the adoption papers."

"What adoption papers? N'yen's? Mine?" Maddy was still not quite awake.

"The Hoople Quadruples. I found the stash of secret papers. Secret Number Three. Maybe Four, Five, and Six."

Maddy swung her feet onto the cold hardwood floor. Careful not to pull the covers off Beau who was snoring quietly on the other side of the four-poster bed.

"Where were they?" she asked, stifling a yawn worthy

of a Gerber's Baby.

"In the vault in the basement."

"There's a vault in the basement?"

"Yes, Bobby helped me find it. We figured it had to be on there – just like the dictionary said – after we found nothing in the cemetery."

"Cemetery? What earth are you talking about?"

"N'yen had already figured it out. He told me to look in the dictionary. So I did. Turns out, the dictionary gave me three choices: A secure room in a bank where valuables are stored. Or a chamber used for burials. Or a strongroom used for storage."

"So?"

"I figured it might be a reference to a bank vault. But I had Aunt Lizzie call someone who worked at the bank to check for any safe deposit boxes rented in the Hoople name. But there weren't any."

"Okay."

"Then we looked inside the Hoople family vault at Pleasant Glades, but found nothing there but a bunch of rusty old caskets. Scratch that."

"You broke into a mausoleum?"

"It was unlocked," she exaggerated.

"And –?"

"So that left 'a large room or chamber used for storage, especially an underground one.' Underground meant the vault had to be in the Mansion's basement. When I got home I made Bobby help me search the rooms down there. We found it first place we looked – hidden behind that big Herring-Hall-Marvin steel safe where I found the birth certificates."

"Behind the safe? How did you manage to move it? That steel safe must weigh 2,000 pounds."

"Fortunately, it has wheels. Safes are moveable; vaults aren't."

"And there's a vault hidden behind the safe?"

"That's what I'm telling you. Together, Bobby and I got that big ol' safe to roll just enough to open the door behind it."

"And you found a vault?

"Well, more of a storage closet. But it had a thick metal door with a combination lock."

"Don't tell me you and Bobby picked the lock?" said Maddy, pulling on her robe and leading her granddaughter to the ante room outside the bedroom. No need to wake Beau. He'd spent the day copying old paintings in his studio. Standing at an easel was exhausting.

"No, I'm not that clever," grinned Aggie. "Turns out, the door was unlocked."

"You're encountering a lot of unlocked doors."

"Just lucky I guess," she said. Hoping no one would attribute the damage to the family mausoleum to her and Bobby.

Her grandmother was more awake now. "Where's Bobby?"

"I sent him home. I didn't want him to miss his 11 o'clock curfew. His dad and my dad agreed we both had to be home by 11 p.m. – remember?"

"Indeed I do. What time is it?"

"Not quite 11:00."

"Okay, you beat the clock," acknowledged Maddy.

"With a few minutes to spare."

Her grandmother said, "May I see what papers you rapscallions found?"

"Of course, Grammy. That's why I woke you." Aggie handed over a gray accordion folder. The label identified it as IMPORTANT DOCUMENTS. "Here you go. I think you're going to be surprised."

"Surprised?"

"Yes. This is Secret Number Three."

Maddy carefully opened the folder and fished her hand inside. She withdrew a sheaf of papers, each bearing the same letterhead: REV. DAVID DIMPLEDORF'S CARING HOME FOR UNWED MOTHERS.

Bingo! The adoption papers.

The documents referred to each of the adoptees by their given names. The adopting parents were listed as Henry and Henrietta Hoople. But the goldmine was the part that identified the birth mother for each child:

```
Hilda:    Barbara Ann König.
Helga:    Arlene Alice Aitkens.
Helena:   Alma Kraft Hankins.
Howard:   Sarah Celine Jinks.
```

~ ~ ~

"Well, I'll be a monkey's uncle," said Aunt Hilda.

"You're actually a König," corrected Aggie. "Not a monkey."

"Really? They're a bunch of lowlifes."

"According to these documents, you're a König," nodded Maddy. She and Aggie had met with the old woman first thing after breakfast to show her the adoption papers.

"This means George König was my birth brother,"

surmised Aunt Hilda. "He was a jerk, a deadbeat, and a petty thief. Leave it to fate that I come from White Trash."

"Not totally," reasoned Aggie. "George and Betty Lou König were the parents of that famous movie star, Missy Montana."

"Oh yes, I'd almost forgotten that. Their daughter Louise went off to Hollywood and became an actress."

"Missy Montana was picked by *People* magazine as one of this year's 50 Most Beautiful People," Aggie pointed out. "That's pretty impressive."

"No wonder you were the prettiest of the Hoople girls," said Maddy. Deliberately flattering the old woman. "You and Missy Montana share the same genes."

"Yes, I supposed that's true."

"Look at this," Aggie turned their attention back to the adoption papers. "Aunt Helena was a Hankins."

"Wasn't Alma Kraft Hankins the mother of Sad Sammy?" asked Maddy. She had trouble keeping family trees straight. That was Cookie's department.

"No," corrected Aunt Hilda. "Alma was Floyd Hankins' mother. Floyd was my sister Helga's boyfriend. But it looks like he was also my sister Helena's brother."

"A coincidence. Nobody knew of the connection back then."

"Besides, he and Helga weren't genetically related," Aggie pointed out. "So if they had got together, it wouldn't be like those inbred Crackletons."

"Aggie! You're a Crackleton."

"Oops. I forgot."

Aunt Hilda tilted her head to consider the matter. "Maybe Helena came by her madness honestly. Alma

Hankins had fits. The family had to lock her in the attic at times."

"That's terrible."

"It was either that or send her to the madhouse."

Maddy's daughter Tilly had wandered into the room, looking for one of Aggie's sisters. The girl had disappeared but no one was particularly concerned. The children were always playing Hide 'n Seek in the Mansion. "Madhouse?" Tilly repeated, puzzled by the conversation. "What madhouse?"

"Back then that would have been Central Indiana Hospital for the Insane," replied Aunt Hilda. "A dreadful place. It was located on South Washington Street in Indianapolis. The state closed it down in the '90s."

Aggie pulled out another adoption certificate. "What about Aunt Helga? It says here she was an Aitkens. Does that mean she was related to Boyd Aitkens?"

"Apparently so," nodded the old woman. "Arlene was Boyd's mother. That would make him and Helga brother and sister. Too bad about him getting blown up by that bomb."

"It wasn't exactly a bomb," said Aggie.

But the old woman wasn't listening. "Poor ol' Boyd. He seemed like a nice enough fellow."

"For a drug dealer," Aggie muttered *sotto voce*.

"What's that —?"

"Nothing. Just a sneeze."

Maddy turned to Aunt Hilda. "Now that you know your true lineage, do you plan to contact Betty Lou König or her daughters?" George had died a dozen years ago, hit by a bolt of lightning during a thunderstorm.

"No, no," she replied. "I've never really cared for Betty Lou. And her daughter Thelma Ann is a no good trollop – doing jail time, thanks to the Quilters Club."

"Sorry about that," Maddy offered an insincere apology.

"Truth is, I wouldn't mind meeting that movie star. What's her stage name again – Mitzy Montana? Yes, she might be an interesting addition to the family."

~ ~ ~

Maddy turned serious. "Now that the Hoople 'family' has expanded, do you plan to redistribute the trust fund money?"

"Too late for that, I'm afraid. Your trust fund and Maisie's are set. I can't touch them."

"I wasn't worried about that."

"And following the tornado I set up the Caruthers Corners Restoration Coalition. That's a done deal. Those millions are helping rebuild the town. So the only money I have left is a small fund that I had Barney Soltairé arrange in order to provide for my ongoing care. That includes Marybelle's salary. And any future medical needs."

There came a sudden *whoo-ee!* from some faraway room, signaling that the two sisters had found Taylor's hiding place. Tilly got up to go check on the children.

"Oh yes," Aunt Hilda added, "there's also a small fund to cover the upkeep of the mansion. I didn't want to put that burden on your family."

"Thank you," Tilly called over her shoulder as she disappeared down the hallway. Although a fanatical neatnik, the old house was much too big even for her obsessive nature.

225

"Yes, thank you," Maddy repeated. A weekly cleaning service had started coming in, putting a shine back on the dusty old structure.

"So you see," Aunt Hilda summed it up, "there's no more money left to distribute. Besides, I doubt a famous movie star like Missy Montana needs my help."

"Probably not," agreed Aggie. "She just got paid $10-million to star in a new movie about Marilyn Monroe." She'd heard that tidbit from Aunt Lizzie, a devout purveyor of Hollywood news. Lizzie Ridenour subscribed to both *Variety* and *The Hollywood Reporter*. Not to mention her bible, *Entertainment Weekly*.

"Haven't there been a zillion movies about Marilyn Monroe?" sighed Maddy. She had really liked the one starring Michelle Williams.

"Apparently they needed one more," smiled her granddaughter. "This one focuses on MM's carrying on with President Kennedy and his brother. *A Family Affair* is the working title, according to the story in *The Hollywood Reporter*."

Maddy ignored her granddaughter's prattle about movies. "So no money goes to the Aitkens family or the other branches?" she asked her aunt.

"None of us had children, other than Howie. That's as far as I'm going – you and your sister Margaret."

"Just checking," Maddy raised her hands to signal defeat.

"Betty Lou König's not getting a dime. And I don't feel any obligation to my fake brother and sisters' relatives," asserted Aunt Hilda. There was a defiant tone to her voice. "I'm the last one standing. Winner take all."

PART IV

While she slept she had a dream. She dreamt that the Neverland had come too near and that a strange boy had broken through from it. He did not alarm her, for she thought she had seen him before in the faces of many women who have no children. Perhaps he is to be found in the faces of some mothers also. But in her dream he had rent the film that obscures the Neverland, and she saw Wendy and John and Michael peeping through the gap.

- *Peter Pan*, J.M. Barrie

Chapter Forty-Three

Adverse Possession

Suzy Aitkens showed up at the Caruthers Corners Police Department, looking like a hiker who had just spotted Sasquatch. "There's a woman living in one of our migrant labor houses," she announced to Myrtle Dobbler, the police dispatcher. Myrtle served as receptionist too.

"What's strange about that? You folks have people in and out of them shacks all the time. You hire more illegal immigrants than Donald Trump's Mar-a-Lago."

"This is a house we don't use anymore. Up near Injun Woods. We're not planting on that field up there, so the house should be empty. But there's an old woman living in it without our permission. I just discovered it this morning. I'm touring all the property to see what I've inherited."

Chief Jim Purdue stepped out of his office, having overheard Suzy's excited voice. "Hello, Miss Aitkens. You say you've got a squatter?"

"I guess that's what you'd call it. Can you send a deputy out to evict her? The nerve of that old woman."

"Did you ask Ralph about it?" He referred to her half-brother, foreman of Aitkens Produce. "Maybe your dad was renting out the place."

"Ralph refuses to talk about it. Like he knows a secret or something. Said to let it go. But I checked with the bookkeeper. Nobody's paying rent on that house."

Jim Purdue rubbed his hand across the smooth dome of his head. An unconscious gesture. Maybe it was preening. After all, Suzy Aitkens was cute as a June bug. "I'll have Petie drive out and take a look-see. Maybe it's some kind of clerical error and this woman's a lawful tenant. Boyd had a dozen or so rental properties at last count."

"Petie? He's the cute deputy?"

"I wouldn't call him that. But his mother might think so."

"He's got a very nice smile."

"I'll send him out to check on your property – smile and all."

"Well, let me know. When I tried to talk with the old woman, she refused to come outside – just kept yelling for me to go away."

~ ~ ~

Deputy Pete Hitzer had trouble finding the migrant labor shack. This northwest corner of the county was largely undeveloped, with few houses and miles of unpaved roads. He drove past the rusty gate to Injun Woods, the campground for Sons of Anthony Wayne, took a right at Jimbo's Big Boulder, a local landmark, then eased along the edge of a fallow watermelon field until he spotted a structure at the farthest end of the Aitkens property.

A large handwritten sign warned STAY OUT! Nevertheless, Petie pulled his police cruiser up to the dilapidated building and honked his horn, signaling for anybody inside to come out.

Nothing moved.

Petie wasn't about to get out of his Dodge Charger. Too easy to get ambushed by some half-crazed migrant squatter. He had no backup. Being a small-town police department, only he and a part-time deputy were on duty today. Plus Myrtle Dobbler and the Chief.

He called in on his radio, informing the dispatcher that the place looked deserted. Suzy Aitkens must be seeing phantoms, he said. Or maybe she had been smoking locoweed. The frizzy-haired girl looked like the free spirit type to him.

"Chief says to try your siren," Myrtle relayed the message. "That should rouse anybody in the vicinity."

"Gimme a sec."

Whooo-oo-oo-ooo.

Myrtle heard the siren sounding its banshee cry over the radio. "Anything?" she asked.

"Wait a sec," said Petie. "I think I seed a curtain move."

Chapter Forty-Four

Not Dead Yet

Petie cautiously stepped out of the cruiser. He studied the shack for a few minutes, then shouted, "This is the police. Come on out. I can see you at the window."

Nothing.

The deputy shifted his weight from foot to foot, a sign of nervousness. "Listen," he shouted. "If you don't come out right now, I'm gonna call for back up. That'll make the Chief very cranky. It won't go well for you if you get arrested for trespassing. One year in jail and a ten thousand dollar fine," he exaggerated. "The judge usually follows the Chief sentencing recommendations. So if you don't cooperate –"

The curtain fluttered. A few minutes later the front door opened with an unoiled screech. An elderly woman, gray hair tied in a bun, was framed by the doorway. She wore a shapeless gingham dress and ankle-high boots. Her face was vaguely familiar, but he couldn't place it.

"Whattaya want?" she demanded.

"Gotta complaint about a squatter. This house belongs to Aitkens Produce. Guess you must be the squatter in question."

The woman frowned, causing the wrinkles in her pale face to look like a wadded-up Kleenex. "I'm no squatter. I bought this place from Boyd Aitkens. Go ask him."

"'Fraid I can't do that, ma'am. Mr. Aitkens is dead."

That stopped her. "When did that happen?"

"A week or so ago. Killed in an explosion."

"How the heck did that happen?"

"Don't ask."

"Well, I bought this house from Boyd 36 years ago. Paid him cash. We shook hands on the deal – and he's lived up to his end of the arrangements."

"What arrangements?" Petie was having trouble following this babble.

"I paid Boyd well for my peace and quiet. He left me alone. Kept the deed in his name as I requested. And now you show up."

"We had a complaint –"

"Was it that stupid little girl who showed up here yesterday? Is she the one who complained about me?"

"That was Suzy Aitkens, Boyd's daughter. She inherited the farm – all the watermelon fields, the warehouses, the main house, even this rundown shack."

"Hmph, guess I haven't kept this place up the way I should. But it's mine. Ask Boyd's boy."

"Ralph?"

"Yes, Ralph. I dunno nothing about no daughter."

"She came on the scene quite recently."

"Spring to life full-grown – like Zeus's daughter Aphrodite?"

"I don't know nobody 'round here named Aphro-whatever. Suzy comes from down near Pitsville."

"Forget Suzy. Go talk to Ralph. He knows about my deal."

"And jus' who are you, ma'am?"

"Helga – Helga Hoople. I've been dead over three decades now. Why couldn't you people just leave me alone?"

Chapter Forty-Five

Return from the Dead

Marybelle Oliver answered the knock at the door. The big brass knocker was shaped like a lion's head, its *clack! clack! clack!* echoing along the dark hallway at the entrance. The Hoople Mansion didn't get many visitors.

"I wonder who that is," Maddy said to Aunt Hilda. They were having afternoon tea in the parlor, a daily routine.

The stout-bodied British woman returned with Police Chief Jim Purdue and his deputy following a few steps behind her. "The bobbies are here," she announced.

"Jim," Maddy greeted her friend, "what brings you to the top of Hoople Hill?"

"A curious thing, to say the least. I'm here to see Miss Hilda."

The old woman looked up. "Yes, Chief Purdue? Something involving me?"

Jim Purdue fidgeted a bit before responding. "Yes ma'am. What I have to tell you is a little hard to believe."

"Well, tell me. Let's see if I believe you."

"We may have found your sister."

"Both Helga and Helena are dead, young man."

"Maybe not. Yesterday, Deputy Hitzer here got a complaint about a trespasser on Aitken Produce property. He found an older woman living in a small house up past

Injun Woods. She claimed she was Helga Hoople."

"Helga – that's impossible," gasped the bird-like woman. "She jumped in that geyser."

"Yes, Jim," echoed Maddy. "You investigated that death yourself, as I recall."

"All the clues pointed to suicide," the police chief defended himself. "The courts ruled her to be deceased. However, no body was ever found."

"Yet, there she was, big as life," declared Petie Hitzer. "Said she's been living up there ever since she disappeared."

"Aunt Hilda's sister still alive?" said Aggie. "This has to be Secret Number Four."

"She's not my sister," muttered the old woman.

"Said she was Helga Hoople," insisted Petie.

"That's not what Aunt Hilda meant," said Maddy. "Did the woman provide any proof of her identity?"

"Yessum. She showed me a driver's license – but it had expired more'n thirty years ago. "But the picture sure looked like a younger version of her."

"How could she have been living in a little shack all these years without anyone knowing?" questioned Maddy. "Surely Boyd Aitkens would have discovered someone living on his land during a lengthy period of time like that."

Jim Purdue responded, "Apparently, she made some kind of off-the-books deal with Boyd Aitkens to buy the property from him. His boy Ralph delivered food and other supplies to her on a monthly basis."

"Problem was," Petie interjected, "no one told Suzy about the arrangement when she took over Aitken Produce. So she thought Miss Helga was a squatter."

"Ralph straightened it out," Jim Purdue finished the

story. "But I thought you should know that your sister's alive and well. If you want to see her, she's up there at her homestead in the middle of nowhere."

Maddy looked around at her aunt and Aggie. "Boyd Aitkens was Helga's biological brother. Do you think he knew about that?"

"How could he?" said Aggie. "I only found those adoption papers last night."

"I'm confused," said the police chief. "You're saying Miss Helga and Boyd were related?"

"Yes. Aggie found the adoption papers last night. Here they are, if you want to see them." Maddy indicated the documents spread across the table. "As you know, my father was the unwanted child of Granny Crackleton. Well, Helga was given up for adoption by Arlene Aitkens."

"Boyd's mom?"

"That's right. The papers also show that Helena came from Alma Hankins. And Aunt Hilda here was given up for adoption by Barbara Ann König."

"Does that make you related to that movie star?" blurted Petie Hitzer. The deputy was obviously star-struck on the beautiful blonde actress.

"Apparently so," the old woman grunted.

"Can you get me an autograph?"

"No, Petie, she can't," said Maddy. "They've never even met each other."

"Awww, shucks."

Jim Purdue was still trying to sort this out in his mind. "Alma Hankins – is that Sad Sammy's mother?"

"No, her sister. Floyd's mother."

"A shame about Floyd getting caught by that twister."

"Yes," agreed Maddy. "Floyd was the best water diviner I ever met."

"A what?" asked her granddaughter.

"A water witcher," explained her Uncle Jim. "Somebody who figures out where to dig a well. Uses a dowsing rod to point to underground water."

"Does that work?"

Jim offered a crooked smile. "Some people believe in it. All I can tell you is that Floyd Hankins had a pretty good track record."

"Floyd helped us find water over at the farm," said Petie. His parents owned Old MacDonald's Dairy. "Dug the well right where he told us and hit an underground spring – zippity-split. What a gusher!"

"Could be that was because there's plenty of underground water around here," smirked Maddy. "It's kinda hard to miss."

"Yeah, but –"

"Back to my sister Helga," snapped the 85-year-old woman. "I don't want to see her. She's been alive for the past 36 years, living 20 miles from here, and never once reached out to let me know I shouldn't be grieving her loss. Shame on her!"

~ ~ ~

Suzy Aitkens took the news well. The trespasser was her aunt – another relative to hang on her family tree like an extra Christmas ornament. Up until recently she didn't know anything about her connection to the Aitkens family of Caruthers Corners. Sure, she'd heard of Aitkens Produce, the big watermelon farm, but she had no idea there was any link other than having the same name.

She'd barely known her father while growing up, a big friendly stranger who sometimes visited on Thanksgiving or showed up for her birthday. He gave her a pony when she turned sixteen and bought her a Mustang GX when she graduated high school. Eventually, she sold the pony, but she still had the Mustang. It was a good, fast car.

He paid her tuition at Indiana Wesleyan. But she didn't really know him. Her mother said they were divorced, although it turned out her mom and dad had never been married.

Suzy had been quite surprised when that lawyer – Harlan Elkins Dingley – had contacted her, saying she needed to come up to Caruthers Corners for the reading of her father's will. She didn't even know he'd died.

Her mom had passed several years ago and her mysterious father's visits had tailed off. She hadn't seen Boyd Aitkens since he'd shown up at her college commencement ceremonies, looking proud and happy. He handed her a check for $10,000. She'd noted it was drawn on an Aitken Produce account, but she didn't give it much thought. No way it could be that big watermelon operation based in Caruthers Corners.

But it was.

Chapter Forty-Six

The Visit

"Let's go call on Helga Hoople," suggested Maddy. She and the Quilters Club had gathered that next morning at Cozy Café to share this new information. Aggie was able to join them because school was closed today for roof repairs.

After serving them all coffee – and a watermelon malt – Maisie Walters pulled up a chair to join the group. After all, she was a certified member of the Hoople family, just like her twin sister Maddy. Helga Hoople was *her* aunt too.

"Why would we want to do that?" asked Bootsie. The matters were settled in her book: The quilt was a copy. Helga had a right to be on the Aitkens property. And so what if she'd faked her own death – Jim wasn't filing charges. Everything was settled.

"Two reasons," persisted Maddy. "One is to find out more details about the Frank Leslie Quilt. According to Rita Rutaberger, Helga made that quilt. Two, to discover why she faked her own death. I suspect there's more to the story than a failed love affair with Floyd Hankins."

"Yes, I definitely want to find out more about that phony quilt," agreed Lizzie between sips of hot coffee. "It sure had me fooled."

"And I want to find out if Helga knew she and Boyd

were brother and sister," said Cookie. Miss Genealogy.

"I'd bet that's why he helped her disappear," offered Maisie.

"We'll see," said Bootsie reluctantly. No way to avoid this wild goose chase.

"How's Aunt Hilda taking these new revelations?" asked Maisie.

"Calm. She already knew they were all adopted, so no shock there. And finding out she was a König was no big deal."

"That's certainly better than being a Crackleton," said Maisie. Not particularly happy with her own new lineage.

"I think she's most upset with Helga," noted Maddy. "Never getting in touch was hurtful. They were pretty close as children, Aunt Hilda says."

"I don't think I'd like being a quadruplet," mused Aggie. "I can barely put up with being one of four children." She wasn't very fond of her sisters. They had never been really close, she told herself. Maybe it was the age difference, the three of them a decade younger than her.

"Being a twin isn't so hard, not if you do it like me and Maddy," joked Maisie. "Separated at birth, we didn't even know we were related till a couple of years ago."

"That's right," Maddy offered a faint smile. "No sibling rivalry. No fighting over clothes. No sharing a room. What's not to like about six decades of never knowing you had a sister?"

"But it's nice to finally discover your true family tree," added Maisie. Unlike Maddy, she'd always known she was adopted.

"Sure it's nice, if it has golden branches like the Hoople

family tree," said Bootsie. "Wish I had a trust fund like you gals."

"Never dreamed I'd have a twin sister … or a trust fund," the café owner batted her eyes with false modesty.

Maddy was glad to have discovered her twin, but her Quilters Club friends were more like true sisters (although she'd never admit that in front of Maisie). "What do you say?" she prompted, glancing at her wristwatch. "Shall we go visit Aunt Helga?"

"I'm game," said Lizzie. Cookie and Aggie nodded. Bootsie was outvoted, as usual.

Maisie heaved a sigh. "You gals go along without me. I have a restaurant to run. Gotta get ready for the lunch rush."

"Okay, I'll give you a full report," promised Maddy.

"Who's driving?" Bootsie was being pouty. "I'm low on gas."

"We can take my car," volunteered Maddy. "That new Navigator will hold every one of you with plenty of room to spare."

"Do you like the Lincoln better than your old Toyota?" asked Lizzie. Status conscious, she drove a Mercedes-Benz.

"So far."

"That monster would be too big for me," commented Cookie. "I would feel like I was driving a battleship."

"Me too," said Aggie. "When I get a car it's going to be something like a Chevrolet Spark or a Ford Fiesta. Something my size." She didn't have her driver's license yet, but Bobby had let her practice-drive his little Fiat Punta. To her it was the difference between a roller coaster and a roller skate.

"Bigger is better," joked Maddy. At 210 inches the Lincoln Navigator was slightly longer than her old Sequoia. "Anything short of a Mack truck better watch out for me."

~ ~ ~

Petie Hitzer couldn't get that girl Suzy out of his mind. She was rude, headstrong, an unabashed dreamer, disrespectful of her sudden position in the community. Not his type at all.

Or was she?

He pictured her heart-shaped face, pouty lips, and frizzy hair – an image that seemed to make his breathing more difficult. What the heck, maybe he'd just ask her out. Worst she could do was laugh in his face.

A gangly ragdoll of a man, he'd been rejected before. He'd had to attend his senior prom alone, a single guy standing with the other losers along the outer wall of the high school auditorium, working up courage to ask a girl to dance.

When he had his first job – a teller at the bank – he'd dated Jane Simpson for a while. Or had it been Jean Simpson? Twins, he was sure they sometimes switched off on him as a practical joke. But that hadn't lasted long. The sisters had been caught up in a scandal with a local history teacher – that very guy they'd had in a jail cell last week at the Caruthers Corners Police Department.

"*Double your pleasure, double your fun,*" townsfolk chanted behind their backs. "Teenage Jezebels," one local minister described them at the time. Jean and Jane now worked at Home Depot, leading a chaste existence from all reports.

Petie's thoughts returned to Suzy Aitkens. She wasn't bad looking. And he liked a girl with spunk, he had to admit. Maybe she *was* his type after all.

One way to find out.

Chapter Forty-Seven

The Purloined Aunt

The morning sun painted the watermelon fields with an orange hue, like an unknown masterpiece by Van Gogh. The shack cast a long shadow that pointed westward. The sun seemed to be balanced on a line of trees in the distance. 10:17 a.m. according to the digital clock on the Navigator's dashboard.

"There it is," pointed Bootsie. She'd gotten the directions from her husband Jim. This place was "way and gone," to use his term. No other houses within miles.

Maddy braked the big SUV, its bone color looking more like ocher in the mid-morning light. "Helga certainly chose to hide out in the middle of nowhere," she observed. "This is the end of the road – literally."

Everybody piled out of the car and gathered at the door of the rundown house. Maddy knocked and called out, "Helga, it's Maddy Madison. I'm your brother Howie's daughter."

"I know who you are," came a voice from inside. "Who's that crowd with you? Those Quilters Club ladies?"

"Yes – Lizzie Ridenour, Cookie Bentley, and Bootsie Purdue. The young girl is my granddaughter Agnes."

"What do you want?"

"To speak with you. Everybody thought you were dead."

"That's the way I wanted it. Leave me to molder in peace."

"I live in the Hoople Mansion with your sister Hilda. The news that you were alive came as quite a shock to her."

"Hilda's not my sister. I assume you know that by now."

"Yes, we found the adoption papers."

"Then you know Boyd Aikens was my younger brother. He helped me escape that phony Hoople Quadruple world. I couldn't take it anymore."

"I'm sure it was hard."

"Nearly fifty years of pretending I was something I wasn't – I'd had enough!"

Maddy leaned closer to the door. "May we come in?"

"I'm not receiving visitors. Up until this week, I hadn't had a visitor in over 30 years. And I liked it that way."

"How do you get supplies – groceries, clothing, toilet paper, things like that?"

"Boyd used to bring them, that was part of the deal. But in recent years his son Ralph has played delivery boy."

"— the deal?"

"When Boyd rescued me from the Hooples – helped me fake my death, that is – he set me up here. Agreed to provide for me. But he was well paid for the services."

Maddy glanced at her companions. "Paid by whom?"

"The Hoople Quadruplets Trust Fund, of course."

Maddy caught her breath. She could feel her heart fluttering like a bird trying to escape its cage. "You're saying Barnabas Soltairé has known all along that you were alive …?"

"Naturally. How else would I get the money to hide out?"

Maddy took a different tact. "We – the Quilters Club, that is – wanted to ask you about that quilt you made as a young woman, the appliqué with women's silhouettes."

Instantly, the door swung open to reveal an older woman wearing a baggy dress and work boots. "Come in," she said. "I'd love to show you my new quilts. They're much better than that old appliqué. I was just a beginner back then."

"Well, uh, okay," Maddy accepted.

Startled by the suddenness of the invitation, the five visitors shuffled into a small living room. The interior of the house was in much better condition than the outside. Everything neatly in its place, like living in a well-planned house trailer. A stuffed round-arm couch and two hardback chairs were arranged around a wooden coffee table. Pictures of birds – reproductions of James Audubon paintings – hung on the walls. A tiny kitchen could be seen off to the right. The other two doors presumably led to the bedroom and a bath.

"You have a nice place," said Cookie, surprised by what she saw. The roughshod woman and the tumbledown outside belied the pristine household.

"Have a seat," Helga Hoople invited. "I'll bring in a couple more chairs from the kitchen."

"Thank you," said Maddy, choosing one of the hardback chairs.

"Shall I make some tea? I hardly know how to behave with visitors. But I do want you to see my quilts."

"We'd like that," said Lizzie. "I head up the Hoople Quilting Heritage Museum."

"Yes, I know. I get the *Burpyville Gazette* with my

monthly deliveries, so I keep up on the news. Not much else to do out here."

"Do you see Barnabas Soltairé often?" inquired Maddy. Still reeling from this new information.

"Heavens no, I haven't seen Barnabas in 36 years, not since I was declared dead."

"How did you find out that you were an Aitkens?" asked Cookie. Trying to connect the genealogical dots.

"Boyd contacted me. His mother told him. She had given me up for adoption some 20 years before he was born, but confessed all when she found out where I was. She recognized me by this tiny port-wine stain birthmark behind my ear." Hilda pulled a lock of her gray hair back to reveal the mark. It was shaped like a half-moon. "She had seen me in a movie newsreel about the famous Hoople Quadruplets of Caruthers Corners."

"Did you ever get to meet her?" asked Lizzie.

"Just before she passed away. Colon cancer it was. Boyd took me to say goodbye. That's when he and I hatched the plan for me to disappear. He hired Jebediah Crackleton to tell everybody that I'd jumped into the geyser."

"We were beginning to think Jeb killed you," said Bootsie. The suspicious cop's wife.

"No, Jebediah spirited me away to this place. Barnabas had purchased the property from Boyd for me, holding the deed in escrow so it couldn't be traced. Then Barnabas advanced the monthly funds for my upkeep – nobody the wiser."

"Why didn't you contact Hilda?" Maddy wanted to know. "She said you two were close as children."

"Not really. She was a needy little thing. Helena was

moody. And Howie was such a little pain, always wanting to play doctor with us girls."

"Your quilts," Lizzie wisely changed the subject. "Your old friend Rita Rutaberger said you only made the one, the appliqué with portraits of women."

"That was true up to about ten years ago. That's when I took up quilting again."

"Why did you do that?" Lizzie pressed.

"Quite frankly, I got bored. I can't pick up a TV signal out here. I've never been able to read, thanks to my dyslexia. I wasn't very good at painting. And I got tired of listening to the radio all the time. Nothing but right-wing talk shows and religious programming. I tried my hand at knitting but couldn't master it, all that knit one, purl two business. Same with crocheting. I'd tried macramé years ago, but didn't like it. That pretty much left quilting."

"Where did you get the idea for that first quilt you made?" asked Bootsie.

"I copied one I saw in a magazine, using images Rita and I collected from old magazines that we found in the basement. But I didn't like appliqué all that much."

"What year was that?"

"Oh, I remember it quite well – 1952. I put the date on the quilt but Rita pointed out that with my dyslexia I'd reversed the numbers. I'd stitched 1925 instead of 1952. I never truly learned to read or write because of that affliction."

"Where are your new quilts?" asked Maddy, just to be polite.

Helga seemed to brighten. "In the shed out back. I call it my sewing room. Come, I'll show you."

Chapter Forty-Eight

Kaleidoscopes

The old woman led them around to the backyard where another structure stood. It looked like an old hen house on the outside, but the interior was just as spiffy as the main house's. Wooden racks positioned around the room displayed dozens of colorful handstitched quilts – a style known as a Kaleidoscope Quilt.

Kaleidoscope quilting dates back to the early 19th Century. Eight identical triangles are sewn together to make an octagon, then four smaller triangles are added to the corners to produce a square block. The angles of the pieces and the arrangement of color creates an optical illusion, looking like the designs you'd find inside a child's toy kaleidoscope.

One particularly magnificent quilt hung on the back wall, its pattern fanning out in all directions, the bright colors dazzling to the eye. The old woman was quite good.

"This is a far cry from that early appliqué quilt," observed Lizzie. Impressed.

"That old quilt I did as a young woman was derivative, a copy of something called the Godey Quilt. These are my own designs. I've varied the traditional Kaleidoscope Quilt a bit, picked my own colors. I find quiltmaking so relaxing. It's a satisfying way to pass the time out here alone."

"So you *do* miss people?" said Cookie.

"I don't miss being part of the Hoople Quadruple circus, always on display – and living a lie. We knew we were fake quads, commercial products created by our adoptive parents. Henry and Henrietta were raking in the bucks and laughing at the gullible people who paid us to endorse their products or make public appearances. We certainly kept ol' Tick Tock busy."

"That was your booker?"

"Yes, I was friends with his daughter Rita. She was a few years younger than me, but we got on fine. We kept in touch until I died."

"You mean faked your death," Maddy gently corrected.

"Claimed my life back, I'd describe it."

"So you've lived out here all alone for over three decades. I wouldn't exactly call that claiming your life back."

"Early on my brother Boyd would visit. He delivered groceries once a month. Even his wife didn't know about me. Then, a few years back, his boy Ralph took over the deliveries. He wasn't interested in talking with some old hermit. Just dropped off the goods and skedaddled."

Bootsie asked, "Did Ralph know you were his aunt?"

"I'm pretty sure he did, but he didn't seem to care one way or t'other. I was just a monthly chore, like feeding the chickens or watering the lawn."

"Do you know how your brother got killed?"

"Blown up, the deputy said. Ralph wouldn't talk about it."

"Blown up in an illegal meth lab."

"Is that some kind of drug?"

"Yes, N-methylamphetamine is a stimulant that affects the central nervous system. Crystal meth looks like glass and is sold on the street by criminals. People use it for recreational highs, but here in Indiana the manufacturing of methamphetamine is a felony with a penalty of up to 10 years in prison and a fine of $100,000," explained Bootsie. Miss Law and Order.

"What was my brother doing in a meth lab?"

"Apparently, he owned it."

"Well, paint me green and call me a pickle. He never told me about owning any meth labs. Just talked about growing watermelons. Why would he get involved in the drug trade? He didn't need the money. Aitkens Produce was worth millions. Not as wealthy as us Hooples, but closing in."

"Someone said the Indianapolis Mob had helped finance his operation. It was a way of laundering money for them."

"Did they blow him up?"

"Probably not. Meth labs are very dangerous. The manufacturing process is one that can cause explosions. The police think it was an accident," replied Bootsie, the voice of authority.

"Oh dear. Now I *am* truly all alone."

"Not really. You still have your nephew Ralph. And Boyd's newly discovered daughter Suzy."

"That little twit who came out here? Where did she come from? Boyd didn't have a daughter."

"It seems she was a love child with a former employee. He left everything to her."

"What about Ralph?"

"Ralph is kinda out in the cold," Lizzie shared the salacious news. "Turns out, he's not really Boyd's son."

"You're saying Ralph's adopted?"

"Not exactly. He's the product of an affair Boyd's wife had. Seems your brother knew about it and punished the boy. Charlie was always his favorite. Or maybe the girl Suzy."

"Then who's Ralph's father?"

"Strangely enough, it was Boyd's partner in the meth lab, a man named Justin Ford Harribald," said Lizzie. Glancing sideways at Cookie. But everything was still calm.

"Who is this Harribald fellow? I've never heard of him." The Hoople Quadruplets had always been home-schooled by tutors. But even if the quads had attended Caruthers High, given the age differences, they would never have crossed paths with Justin Ford Harribald.

"Actually, he's our old high school history teacher," confessed Cookie. "We were all in his class."

Everybody offered an embarrassed smile, as if guilty by association. But studying history under a future drug dealer couldn't possibly be counted as a crime.

"Manufacturing illegal drugs seems like an unusual sideline for a schoolteacher," muttered the old woman. Her head reeling with all this new information. She obviously hadn't received a recent delivery of *Burpyville Gazettes* – missing coverage of her brother's death or the history teacher's arrest.

"He said he got the idea from a TV show called *Breaking Bad*."

"That means nothing to me. I haven't seen a television show in over thirty years. Like I said, I get no reception out here."

"You haven't missed much," nodded Cookie, not a big fan of television programming. She had never forgiven the History Channel for veering away from its World War Two shows ("The Hitler Channel," she'd called it) to the current drivel about flying saucers and bigfoot.

"There's no reason for you to keep living such a reclusive life," coaxed Maddy. "The Hoople Quadruples are no more. The secret will come out. And the only other living member is your sister Hilda."

"I told you, she's not really my sister."

"Maybe you weren't quadruplets, but you were adopted brother and sisters. Raised together as a family. Why don't you move into the Hoople Mansion with us? There's still an empty wing."

"You'd have me?"

"You're my aunt," said Maddy.

"As much as Hilda is, I suppose," said the elderly woman.

"That's why you should move back to the Mansion. Isn't that right, Aggie?"

"More the merrier," grinned the girl. Her family having just enlarged by one.

Chapter Forty-Nine

Murder Most Foul

Barnabas Soltairé confirmed the arrangement Boyd Aitkens had with his sister. Per Helga's instructions, Soltairé was holding her deed to the little parcel of land in escrow. No records to show she was still alive.

Soltairé also confirmed Helga had a separate trust fund that paid for everything – groceries, electricity, you name it. Turned out, these payments were clearly accounted for in the umbrella trust's financial statements, but Aunt Hilda had never bothered to look. The old woman never concerned herself with such details, merely making her wishes known to Barnabas and leaving the accounting to him.

Respecting Helga's wishes, he'd never told Hilda about her sister's existence.

When confronted by Police Chief Purdue, he was more than happy to explain it all – the secret adoptions, Helga's disappearance, financial details of the various trusts. With his client's okay he was free to talk. And that client was now Madelyn Agnes Hoople Taylor Madison. Hilda and Helga had agreed to give her Power of Attorney over their affairs. A heavy burden off their shoulders.

Maisie was good with it too. She preferred the simple life of running her diner and making random acts of charity with her fat trust fund. Maddy could have her proxy.

Chief Purdue had lots of questions. As did Mark the Shark. Barnabas Soltairé was very cooperative, explaining the Hoople family history, the trust funds, how he had watched over the quadruplets for the past forty years. A side job after he graduated law school, but full time in recent years.

But when asked about the Mob's financing of Aitkens Produce, Soltairé clammed up. "Attorney-client privilege," was his only statement about that. In a way, affirming Sal Molino's involvement with the watermelon farmer.

Police Chief Jim Purdue turned the matter over to the FBI. Special Agent in Charge Neil "The Nailer" Wannamaker confirmed that they had long suspected Boyd Aitkens of laundering money for Sal Milano, but could never prove it.

"Suzy has offered to turn over the books," said Chief Purdue. "That oughta help."

"Is she a straight arrow?"

"Yeah – kind of a high-minded hippie. She's talking about turning Aitkens Produce into a town-owned enterprise. A co-op. Power to the people and all that."

"Doesn't she realize she's now a wealthy woman, head of one of the largest produce empires in the state?" said SAC Wannamaker. "That's a lofty position for a 26-year-old woman. And a lot to turn over to the townspeople of Caruthers Corners."

"Doesn't care. I hear she's gonna have Ralph run the new co-op."

~ ~ ~

Maddy had a different opinion. "Suzie had better find

another foreman," she said when Jim Purdue repeated the conversation that night over dinner. The Quilters Club and their spouses had gathered for a Super Supreme (actually, three of the 14" pies) at the Pizza Hut on Highway 21. Aggie had been invited along, because she was moping over N'yen's return to Chicago.

Jim looked up, a wedge of pizza crammed halfway in his mouth. "Why's that?" he mumbled, trying to chew and talk at the same time. The combination of pepperoni, ham, beef, pork sausage, Italian sausage, red onions, mushrooms, green peppers and black olives was a favorite with this gang of old friends.

"Because you're going to arrest Ralph for murder," she replied between bites.

The police chief looked puzzled. "Murder of who?"

"Boyd Aitkens. He and Justin Harribald set Boyd up to die in that meth lab explosion."

Jim Purdue lowered his slice of Super Supreme into the plate, his appetite suddenly sidetracked. "How do you figure that?"

"N'yen hacked into Boyd Aitkens' email. There was a message from Ralph asking his dad to meet him 'at the lab' that day. That's why Boyd was there. And why Ralph and Justin weren't. Tommy D dropped Boyd off at Mr. Harribald's apartment. The door was open but no one was there."

"You're saying your grandson hacked into a private email account?"

"I'm surprised you hadn't already subpoenaed Boyd's email records."

"We didn't think we needed to. It was an open-and-shut

case of accidental death."

"But it wasn't," said Maddy. "Ralph had learned Justin Harribald was his biological father. The two of them concocted a plan to kill off Boyd so Ralph would inherit everything and share it with his real dad. But as it turned out those two bozos didn't know about Suzy. She was the wild card."

Jim Purdue remained fixated on his oversight. "I can't believe that little rascal hacked into Boyd's email. That's illegal, y' know."

"C'mon, Jim," Beau slapped him on the shoulder. "If you'd thought of checking Boyd's emails you would've had to hire someone like N'yen to do it for you. Just pretend he was working as a technical consultant for the Police Department and send him a check for services rendered. I'm sure Mark will approve the expenditure."

"Well –" He knew Tommy Truehart could have checked those emails, but he'd told him not to bother. His gaffe.

"Keep focused," advised Jim's wife. "The important thing is we've just exposed a murder plot. Boyd's death wasn't an accident."

"But how did they set off the explosion? Ralph was at the farm with about twenty migrant laborers as witnesses. And a dozen people saw Justin Harribald at Food Lion."

"Remember that lump of wax you found at the scene of the explosion?" said Maddy. "Freddie told me about it. That was likely a candle. Easy to light a candle and let it burn down to where it ignites a fuse. That meth concoction would blow at the slightest spark."

Edgar spoke up. "I never did trust that Ralph Aitkens. He always seemed kinda weaselly to me."

"Took after his biological father," muttered Cookie. She had pretty well accepted that her god had clay feet. No more hero worship for her old history professor. She was over him, memories discarded – as much as an eidetic mind could discard memories.

Her husband Ben said, "I'll bet it was a heckuva shock when Ralph found that killing Boyd was all for nothing – that he'd been cut out of the will."

"Crime doesn't pay," muttered Jim Purdue, as if repeating a mantra he lived by.

"Do you think Justin Harribald will still get a free pass with that Witness Protection Program?" asked Edgar. "Seems like a pretty sweet deal."

"Don't know if the Organized Crime Task Force will let him walk on a murder charge ... but f'sure he'll talk a lot more rather than jeopardize a possible Get Out of Jail Free card. He'll roll over on Ralph."

"On his own son?"

"Like you said, that Witness Protection Program is a pretty sweet deal."

"Well, there you have it," said Maddy. "Ralph and Mr. Harribald murdered Boyd Aitkens for his farm, but it wound up in the hands of an unknown daughter."

Beau Madison patted his wife on the shoulder with admiration. "Way to go, hon."

She smiled at him. "Thanks, Pooh Bear. But you're asking N'yen to look at Boyd's email is what confirmed our suspicions."

Beau chuckled. "He's a good boy. Might make a famous computer scientist someday – if he doesn't go to jail for hacking the Pentagon."

"The Pentagon?" said Jim Purdue.

"Just kidding."

"I've gotta make a phone call," said the police chief. "To tell Petie to pick up Ralph Aitkens for the murder of his father."

"Boyd wasn't really his father," Bootsie reminded her husband. "Mr. Harribald was."

"His partner in crime," Lizzie nodded.

"Nobody in this town seems to be who they think they are!" he exclaimed.

"Maybe not – but that's no excuse for murder," said Maddy.

"Don't worry," Jim vowed as he dialed his deputy. "He'll pay for his misdeeds. I'll see to that."

"Dibs on that last piece of pizza," said Bootsie.

"No way," countered Maddy. "You have to split it with me."

"Oh, all right."

But when they reached for the piece, someone had already snagged it. "Looks like the Quilters Club has solved another case," said Aggie as she ate the last slice of pizza.

Epilogue

Justin Ford Harribald was important enough as a witness against the Indianapolis Mob that the Feds gave him a pass on the murder charge. After all, the victim had been a criminal co-conspirator, no great less to society in the FBI's viewpoint. So the former history teacher wound up in some retirement home in a small town, and Ralph took the fall.

Harribald likely didn't end up in Miami Beach. Federal prosecutors took a secret glee in parking criminals in places they would hate, say, working in a shoe store in Great Falls, Montana. Harribald was probably tucked away in some shoddy eldercare facility in Akron, Ohio, or Kalamazoo, Michigan.

Ralph Waldo Aitkens got 65 years at Indiana State Prison. The max for premeditated murder. His dad left him holding the bag by turning state's evidence.

Teddy D got a one year sentence at Pendleton, the juvenile correction facility down in Madison County. That was his reward for cooperation, better than the 20 to 30 years he would have been facing if tried as an adult.

Teddy's Infiniti QX60 was sold at auction to James Elwood. An upgrade for his son Bobby. The little '98 Fiat Punta had been on its "last legs" – or wheels as the case may be.

Helga Hoople took up residence in the Hoople

Mansion, reuniting with her adopted sister. There was plenty of room for everyone. It was like living in a large apartment building. Chief Jim Purdue elected not to pursue any charges re Helga faking her own death. "Who cares after all these years," he opined when being interviewed by WZUR radio. Mayor Mark Tidemore backed him up. "Caruthers Corners is a town of new beginnings," he'd said when asked to make a statement.

After getting over her snit, Aunt Hilda embraced the return of Helga. There was too much family history to ignore. The two remaining "quadruplets" hired a ghostwriter to help them pen a tell-all book, tentatively titled *The Great Quad Con.* Random House had agreed to publish it. They donated the $100,000 advance to the Caruthers Corners Restoration Coalition.

Lizzie Ridenour scheduled an exhibit of Helga's Kaleidoscope Quilts at the museum. Not a historical scoop like she'd expected with the Frank Leslie Quilt, but this new show would get a lot of attention due to Hilda Hoople's well-publicized "Return from the Dead." The Hoople Quadruples were news again!

Cookie Bentley seemed to exorcize the ghosts of her past, putting her relationship Justin Ford Harribald behind her. She busied herself with authenticating a newly discovered journal of Ferdinand Aloysius Jinks. Along with Jacob Abernathy Caruthers and Col. Beauregard Hollingsworth Madison, Jinks had been one of the Town Founders. If true, the journal contained some rather startling information about the early days of Caruthers Corners.

Maddy Madison had come across the Jinks journal in

the library of the Hoople Mansion. Apparently, Henry and Henrietta Hoople had been serious collectors of rare books and other historic memorabilia. The library was proving to be a treasure trove. Cookie was spending one day a week there, searching the shelves.

N'yen received a $500 check for his "consultation services" to the Caruthers Corners Police Department and a silver badge declaring him an HONORARY DEPUTY. The boy used the money to buy a *Vampirella* #1. The rare 1969 Warren magazine featured the cover art of Frank Frazetta. He thought the female vampire was sexy. Puberty in action. He might be a genuine genius, but he was still a teenage boy.

Aggie, as good as her word, let Bobby Elwood put his hand inside her blouse, but she refused to let him slip it under her training bra. Maybe next time, she told herself. Her mom would kill her if she ever found out about this indiscretion. Her mom could be such a spoilsport.

Speaking of dating, Petie Hitzer was now going out with Suzy Aitkens. A whirlwind romance, they were talking marriage. Apparently, she found dairy farming more interesting than watermelon growing. Petie's parents were planning to retire to Florida, leaving Old MacDonald's Dairy in Petie's care. He had submitted his resignation as a deputy.

Chief Purdue had offered the open position to Matea Davis, the young Potawatomi who managed the local Dollar General. Matea was interested, for the policing job would be less confining than that of a store manager. As an Native American, he liked being outdoors. A heritage thing, he said.

With Helga's urging, her new niece turned the

management of the just-formed Aitkens Produce Co-Op over to Barnabas Soltairé. A capable man, he could handle the Hoople Quadruplets Trust Fund with one hand, the Co-Op with the other, and still find time to take Sal Milano's phone calls from Leavenworth.

The Feds busted Sal the Whisper for drug trafficking, based on Mr. Harribald's testimony. The mobster was looking at 20 years to life. Although Justin Harribald disappeared into the Federal Witness Protection Program, word on the street said he had a $100,000 price on his head, courtesy of the Indy Mob.

Beau Madison went in with his pal Edgar Ridenour and bought a new boat, a 20-foot Roughneck 2070 SC. Price tag: $21,499. Having a wife with a big fat trust fund was a good thing, he decided.

N'yen would be surprised, come next visit.

Lizzie's daughter got a divorce. She'd started calling her mother for the first time in years. Lizzie and Edgar had never truly liked their daughter's slacker husband in the first place. He'd been a major source of the family's estrangement.

Bootsie's animal shelter got an anonymous donation of $200,000. That would build several new kennels. Maddy was fond of dogs. Aggie's little pup followed her room-to-room around the Mansion when his mistress was off at school. Tige wasn't fond of other dogs.

Maddy's son Bill got an anonymous donation of $200,000 also, badly needed funds that would keep the doors open on his children's service for another year. He and Kathy were doing good work. N'yen was lucky to have them as parents.

Freddie received cosmetic surgery on his face, thanks to his mother's largess. He still looked like a refugee from a horror flick, but the scar tissue was reduced greatly. The skin graft came off his buttocks, making sitting down kinda dicey for several weeks. His wife playfully called him "butt face."

Tilly said there was nothing in the world she wanted, that her life was "just perfect." She was happy "living in a fairy tale castle." Even so, she didn't object when Maddy set up college funds for the Trio of Trouble that matched Aggie's.

Determined to treat all her grandchildren equally, Maddy arranged a college fund for Freddie's daughter too. Fair was fair.

~ ~ ~

Cookie got the report back from Maryland Biological Analytics. It had compared Maddy's DNA with the other samples collected in Crackleton Crossing by the Geographical Society of Baltimore. It matched her with Granny Crackleton. But the big surprise was the connection with another residents of that out-of-the-way outpost: Dirty Dean Winslow, a reputed cousin of James Dean. There was a 92% likelihood that he was her grandfather.

~ ~ ~

Thanksgiving dinner was a big to-do this year. Everybody was invited to the Hoople Mansion, its dining room large enough to accommodate hordes of friends and neighbors. Many people came just to see the inside of the old stone monolith. Three turkeys were served. The long mahogany side table was crowded with towering mounds of dirty mashed potatoes, candied sweet potatoes simmering in melted brown sugar, roasted ears of yellow corn with butter, and slices of jellied cranberry. A dozen watermelon pies lined the nearby dessert table.

Aunt Hilda and Aunt Helga were giddy on hard apple cider. The kids were drinking watermelon tea. Beau made a toast that was memorable, something about being thankful for good friends and the blessings of living in a small town like Caruthers Corners. The guests shouted, "Here! Here!" as they raised their glasses. It was a great celebration!

Beauregard Hollingsworth Madison IV died two days later.

How this tragedy happened – Beau's murder, the big robbery, and the secret of the Town Founders – is related in the next Quilters Club mystery.

List of Characters
in
A Thimbleful of Murder

The Quilters Club

- Madelyn "Maddy" Madison, de facto head of the Quilters Club.
- Elizabeth "Lizzie" Ridenour, head of Hoople Quilting Heritage Museum.
- Katherine "Cookie" Bentley, head of Caruthers Corners Historical Society.
- Barbara "Bootsie" Purdue, head of local animal shelter.

Quilters Club (Junior Members)

- Agnes "Aggie" Tidemore, Milly and Mark Tidemore's 15-year-old daughter. Maddy and Beau's granddaughter.
- N'yen Madison, Bill and Kathy Madison's adopted 13-year-old Vietnamese son. Maddy and Beau's genius grandson.

The Husbands

Beauregard Hollingsworth Madison IV, retired mayor. Great grandson of a Town Founder.

- Edgar Ridenour, retired bank president.
- Ben Bentley, retired farmer. Head of Sons of Anthony Wayne.
- Jim Purdue, Caruthers Corners Police Chief.

Maddy's Children

- Bill and Kathy Madison, heads of a children's shelter in Chicago. N'yen's adoptive parents.
- Freddie and Amanda Madison, local fire chief and his wife. Donna Ann's adoptive parents.
- Milly and Mark Tidemore, town's mayor and his wife. Parents of Aggie and her three younger sisters ("Trio of Trouble").

Hoople Quadruples

- Hilda Hoople, last surviving member of Hoople Quadruplets. Maddy's aunt.
- Helga Hoople, a Hoople Quadruplet. Committed suicide.
- Helena Hoople, a Hoople Quadruplet. Died in an asylum.
- Howie Hoople, a Hoople Quadruplet. Died from poisoning. Maddy and Maisie's biological father.
- Maisie Walters, Maddy's separated-at-birth fraternal twin sister. Owner of Cozy Café.
- Sue Ann Polk, Maddy and Maisie's late mother.
- Emily Polk, Sue Ann Polk's sister. Suffering from Alzheimer's.

Hoople Staff

- Marybelle Oliver, Aunt Hilda's British-born caregiver.
- Barnabas "Barney" Soltairé, former mob lawyer. Administrator of the Hoople Quadruples Trust Fund.
- Molly Soltairé, one-time Hoople Family maid. Barnabas's mother. Now deceased.
- Thomas "Tick Tock" Dockery, booker of appearances for Hoople Quadruplets. Now deceased.

Aggie's Friends

- Robert "Bobby" Elwood, Aggie's boyfriend.
- Joan "Joanie" McPhee, Aggie's BFF.
- Pricilla "Prissy" Moretz, Aggie's BFF.
- Theodore "Teddy" DiMacchio, A/K/A Teddy D, Pricilla's boyfriend.

Pets

- Tige, Aggie's dog, a wire-haired Dachshund mix.
- Inka, Dinka, and Doo, Bootsie's three rescued dogs.
- Alexander the Great, Mrs. Warton's cat. Now owned by Maisie Walters.

Aitkens Produce

- Boyd Aitkens, head of Aitkens Produce, the largest watermelon farm in the county.

- Ralph Aitkens, Boyd's oldest son. Foreman of Aitkens Produce.
- Charlie Aitkens, Boyd's youngest son. Now deceased.
- Susan Quinlan Aitkens, Boyd's illegitimate daughter. Known to friends as "Suzy Q."
- June Aitkens, Boyd's wife. Now deceased.
- Arlene Alice Aitkens, Boyd's mother. Now deceased.
- Marlene Jurgens, Suzy's mother. Now deceased.
- Louise Gluck, Aitkens Produce staff accountant.

Law Enforcement

- Pete "Petie" Hitzer, police deputy. Parents own Old McDonald's Dairy.
- Tommy Truehart, police deputy. Lives with aunt. Master online gamer known as Beelzebub666.
- Myrtle Dobbler, police dispatcher. Elvina's sister.
- Elvina Dobbler, police dispatcher. Myrtle's sister.
- Frank Crenshaw, Burpyville Police Chief
- Herman Vox, Burpyville crime scene tech.

Neil "The Nailer" Wannamaker, FBI Special Agent in Charge for Indianapolis.

Various Townspeople

- Jasper Beanie, Town Hall custodian, cemetery caretaker, town drunk.
- Thelma Ann König, worked at Dairy Queen. Now in prison.
- Louise Carol König, Thelma's big sister. Now an A-list movie star known as Missy Montana.
- Betty Lou König, Louise and Thelma Ann's mother.
- George König, Betty Lou's husband and Barbara Ann König's son. Now deceased.
- Barbara Ann König, George's mother. Now deceased.
- James Elwood, Bobby's dad. Manager at Home Depot.
- Jean Simpson, a clerk at Home Depot. Identical twin sister of Jane Simpson.
- Jane Simpson, a clerk at Home Depot. Identical twin sister of Jean Simpson.
- Rita Rutaberger, an elderly widow living on an IBM pension.
- Sad Sammy Hankins, a watermelon farmer.
- Alma Kraft Hankins, Sammy's aunt, Floyd's mother. Now deceased.
- Dr. Randall Orange, DDS. A local dentist.
- Francine Jenkins, Avon sales lady.
- Herbie Benson, a local stoner.
- Ronald "Buddy" Flynn, owner of Flynn's Texaco.

- Margaret "Margie" Yost, owner of hairstyling salon in Burpyville.
- Bob "Flash" Dougan, photographer.
- Matea Davis, a Potawatomi Indian. Sons of Anthony Wayne troop leader, manager at Dollar General.

The Meth Dealers

- Justin Ford Harribald, a retired history teacher.
- Floyd Hankins. Helga Hoople's one-time boyfriend. Now deceased.
- Joseph "Little Joe" Flynn, Buddy's younger brother.
- George "Possum" Johnson, a local hermit.
- Salvatore Milano, head of the Indianapolis Mob. Known as Sal the Whisperer.

The Crackletons

- Sarah Celine "Granny" Crackleton, matriarch of the Crackleton Clan.
- Ed Crackleton, Granny's younger brother. Father of numerous delinquents.
- Jebediah Crackleton, Granny's son, a giant in size, serving time in prison.
- Claude Crackleton, Granny's other son. A special needs case.
- Faith Ann Ritchie, Granny's daughter. Mother of Gus and several other kids. Currently managing the Jiffy Mart.

- Augustus "Gus" Crackleton, one of Faith Ann's numerous children. Cookie and Ben Bentley's foster son.

Lawyers

- Harlan Elkins Dingley, Esq., a new lawyer in town. Grandson of the late Bartholomew Dingley. Esq., who was Mark Tidemore's mentor.
- J. Harold Wentworth, Esq., a shady lawyer from Burpyville.
- The Honorable John Lawrence Bristol, a corrupt judge and Wentworth's uncle.
- The Honorable Harry Cramer, a go-to jurist.

Other Historic Figures

- Mildred Potter Lissauer (1897–1998), famous appliqué quilter. Creator of the Godey Quilt.
- Martha Potter (unknown), Mildred's mother.
- Frank Leslie (1821-1880), publisher of *Leslie's Weekly*. Birth name, Henry Carter.
- Louis Antoine Godey (1804-1878), publisher of *Godey's Lady's Book*, the first successful women's fashion magazine.
- Sarah Josepha Hale (1788-1879), editor of *Godey's Lady's Book*. Author of "Mary Had a Little Lamb."

- Amelia Earhart (1897-1937), first female pilot to fly solo across the Atlantic.
- Rev. David Arthur Dimpledorf (1928-2016), disgraced televangelist. Known as "Rev. Dimple." Head of the Forever Family Foundation. Murdered by an irate parishioner.

Caruthers Corners Founding Fathers

- Col. Beauregard Hollingsworth Madison.
- Jacob Abernathy Caruthers.
- Ferdinand Aloysius Jinks.

End Notes

The references to the Godey Quilt are accurate, a unique quilt created in 1934 by Mildred Potter Lissauer (1897–1998) of Louisville, Kentucky.

There is in fact an Illiana Watermelon Association, but it's used fictionally in this story.

References to *Leslie's Weekly* and *Godey's Lady's Book* are factual. Same for their eponymous publishers. And the covers described herein actually exist.

The types of aberrant memory conditions described herein are based on medical descriptions. However, I can't remember what I had for breakfast yesterday.

There was a Geographical Society of Baltimore that conducted an 886-page study of the Bahama Islands in 1903. They never looked at Indiana communities.

The information about N-methamphetamine (and how to make it) is correct to the best of my knowledge, although I've never actually seen a meth lab. They sound dangerous to me, not to speak of the damage their product wreaks on society.

All the quilt styles mentioned in this book – Drunkard's Path, Disappearing Nine Patch, La Passacaglia, Bear's Claw, Celtic Knot, Kaleidoscope, as well as the appliqué designs – are real, and I recommend them to serious quilters.

- Marjory Sorrell Rockwell

Thank you for reading.
Please review this book. Reviews
help others find Absolutely Amazing eBooks and
inspire us to keep providing these marvelous tales.
If you would like to be put on our email list
to receive updates on new releases,
contests, and promotions, please go to
AbsolutelyAmazingEbooks.com and sign up.

Bonus

If you will go to the Absolutely Amazing eBooks online bookstore (AbsolutelyAmazingEbooks.com) and enter the password below into the Bonus Reward Section, you can access recipes for many of the dishes you read about in this book – for free!

AA1062

About the Author

Marjory Sorrell Rockwell says needlecraft arts – quilting, crocheting, knitting – are pastimes every woman can appreciate. And she particularly loves quiltmaking. "It's like painting with cloth," she says. But when not quilting she writes mysteries about a Midwestern sleuth not unlike herself, a middle-aged lady with an unpredictable family and loyal friends. And she's a big fan of watermelon pie.

www.ingramcontent.com/pod-product-compliance
Lightning Source LLC
Chambersburg PA
CBHW070443030726
47503CB00004B/862